Lois Bender
Empire, MI

THE WOMEN'S WARRIOR SOCIETY

THE WOMEN'S
WARRIOR SOCIETY

LOIS BEARDSLEE

THE UNIVERSITY OF ARIZONA PRESS   TUCSON

The University of Arizona Press

© 2008 Lois Beardslee

Library of Congress Cataloging-in-Publication Data

Beardslee, Lois.

The women's warrior society / Lois Beardslee.

p. cm. — (Sun tracks ; v.62)

ISBN 978-0-8165-2671-0 (alk. paper) —

ISBN 978-0-8165-2672-7 (pbk. : alk. paper)

1. Indian women—North America—Fiction.

2. Experimental fiction. I. Title.

PS508.15w66 2008

813'.6—dc22   2007027599

Publication of this book is made possible in part by
the proceeds of a permanent endowment created
with the assistance of a Challenge Grant from the
National Endowment for the Humanities, a federal
agency.

Manufactured in the United States of America on
acid-free, archival-quality paper containing a mini-
mum of 50% post-consumer waste and processed
chlorine free.

13 12 11 10 09 08   6 5 4 3 2 1

CONTENTS

THE WOMEN'S WARRIOR SOCIETY

BABY STEALERS (BY NIGHT)

One might think that they come in the night. Occasionally
    they do. But those nighttime baby stealers are
        gentler. They give the stolen ones back to their
families in the forms of memories and heartbreak and the
    need to help one another. They give them back to the
        anguished mothers, to the culture, to eternity.
They allow those babies to slowly, painfully slide from one
    memory into another, allow them to take on new forms,
        as stars, as snowflakes, as auroras, as sudden,
shifting night winds, as faint squeaking sounds in a
    distant corner of a house, as tears and swollen,
        stiff nostrils and cheeks.

Those nighttime baby stealers got a lot of history and
    precedent to eventually, after decades and lifetimes
        and a half, break trail for brief bits and
moments of peace, acceptance, and acknowledgment of loss.
    Those nighttime baby stealers, they're the ones we've
        known about, dreaded, prayed against, prayed to,
prayed for the strength to educate ourselves away from, to
    run away from, to hide frozen-in-time-and-space from.
        One might think that we hate them, treat them as
enemies, curse them, and mal-name them. But they are among
    us and always have been. We try to avoid them. We tell
        stories about them. We build traditions about
them. We create histories about them. We name them. We

teach prevention about them. We build frightening
stories to ward off interaction with them. We
build stories of beauty and towering trees and skies to
console and nurture ourselves after we confront them.

And it is by this means that we coax and woo and coerce
them into giving our babies back to us. They return
them to us, eventually, as stars, as snowflakes,
as auroras, as sudden, shifting night winds, as faint
squeaking sounds in a distant corner of a house, as
tears and swollen, stiff nostrils and cheeks.
They give them back to anguished family members, to whole
cultures, to eternity.

BABY STEALERS (BY DAY)

They came by horse-drawn wagon, over roads rutted, frozen
in mud slick as mucous membranes, but rock hard and
easier to traverse than the slime of summer clay.
They came over sand-blown trails that existed only by
virtue of the fringe of dune and prairie grasses and
herb-flowers that remained outside the vacant
paths where vegetation was killed and vegetation had
already been scant.

They came over root-bordered two-tracks that tossed the
hell-bound thieves from side to side, from tall
treetrunk to tall treetrunk. They came over
rotting corduroy swamp paths, curving, ascending, begging
for dry ground and scratched and grasped at every
angle by brush and undergrowth.

And in escape, the Indians danced the risky dance they had
no choice but to dance with the baby stealers of the
night. They slipped as quietly into oblivion as
they possibly could. They slipped into places so remote
that the creaking, moaning, suffering wagons of wood
and perspiration could not reach them. They
nurtured their babies and cuddled their babies. They found
food, made shelter, rebuilt entire civilizations and
redefined culture.

And still they came, on horseback, strapping adolescent
        girls and their younger charges to the jagged back
                mounts of store-bought beasts. Grabbing
ambulatory children from their mothers' unaware grasps—at
        their cooking fires, on forages for summer fruits, on
                joyful, playful expeditions away from the men and
the elders who hunted, built, kept watchful eyes in as many
        directions as possible. Or they took children at
                gunpoint, disenfranchising gaping fathers
and uncles and grandfathers, disrupting their thinning
        hopes at building their places in the only societies
                they ever knew . . . again . . .

And they came by bushplane, creeping up to moose-tracked
        beaches of abundance and long-time comfort, wooing the
                unsuspecting children from their ignorant mothers
with sweets and technology. Or water-skidding into whole
        towns of disruption and starvation and desperation,
                bullying the relocated into letting go of their
most prized possessions because they did not have the
        strength left in their limbs to cling. They could do
                nothing but stare up at the sky and wonder when
and if their babies would come back.

They could do nothing but stare into the trembling bushes
        and wonder when and if their babies would come back.
                They could do nothing but stare across the
barren, empty spaces and wonder if their babies were still
        alive from one minute to the next. If their babies
                would reappear like the miracles of the

inevitable sunrise or stars on clear, cold nights — or the
   turn of the seasons, the falling and regrowth of
      leaves, the build-up and recession of ices and
snows, the slowness and stiffness of old age. There was no
   cultural confirmation in all of this, no realization
      that those babies were dead or gone to join their
ancestors and loved ones. No confirmation of their presence
   in the stars, in the snowflakes, in the auroras, in
      sudden, shifting night winds, in faint, squeaking
sounds in a distant corner of a house, as tears, as
   swollen, stiff nostrils and cheeks. No one knew if
      they would be returned to anguished family
members, to whole cultures, to eternity.

Kill the Indian. Save the man. Destroy the family.
   Eventually, destroy hope. Leave them there, with open,
      empty arms, those family members. Leave them
there, with mouths hanging open, not able to think of
   anything but their missing babies, not knowing if the
      air they involuntarily sucked in was too hot or
too cold. Not knowing if the wind or the rain or the snow
   or the darkness or relentless heat beat upon their
      empty-shell bodies like pounding waves or
sandstorms or wretched, jagged hail. Terrified. Waiting.

Some came back. Long, loooong — loooooong — after hope and
   empty motions and wasted days and nights and months
      and years of pacing, sitting, wasting, wondering
what, what to do next. Some came back as bodies. Some came
   back as stories of bodies, bodies never seen, the kind

that do not become stars or auroras, the kind
that live out eternity as unpredictable and shifting winds,
        leaving mothers' arms wanting and unsure of finality.
        Some came back as empty shells, abused beyond
recovery, walking like ghosts of former Indian children,
        fighting and angry like ghosts of former Indian
                children, sexually dysfunctional like former
Indian children. Young men who could not hunt. Young women
        who could not mother. It was like losing them all over
        again.

That's what it was like, when the baby stealers of the
        daylight sent home, if anything, only empty shells,
                only bits and pieces of Indian children. Yeah,
that's what it was like.

One would think that they would get used to it, those
        Indians, every time a child escaped and was sent back,
                every time there was a reprieve and a lucky child
was sent back for a birth, for a death, for a ceremony, for
        a summer, for a weekend. One would think that those
                Indian mothers and fathers and all of those other
family members would get used to the idea that their
        children had to be improved and adapted to meet the
                needs of the dominant society. One would think
that they could let go. But it didn't work that way. Those
        mothers, they cried empty-heart-and-arm cries echoing
                into the nights and against the trees across the
lake and against the stars above the prairies and against
        the sun and the wind and the empty spaces that used to

be filled with the future. They clawed and they grasped and they lunged and they wept and they clung until their fingernails tore every time their babies were wrenched away from them and tied to the back haunches of a horse, or heaved, writhing, onto a horse-drawn wagon, shoved into a plane, a train, or the dark and soul-less Indian-child-eating bowels of a public school bus.

BABY STEALERS (BY PREJUDICE)

There is no way to know in advance. Racism, stupidity, hatred, hunger for power—they do not come with road signs. They do not come with billboards. They do not come with flashing lights. They do not come with blaring horns, attention-grabbing sirens, GONNA HURT YOU written backwards so that we can see it in a rearview mirror. Abusers do not necessarily come in a different cloth from the common man. They do not necessarily come with their intentions posted on their foreheads, etched upon their long-toothed trickery, which is unspoken in the silent, beckoning motions of their hands.

Abusers are born of tradition, tradition of history, tradition of eminent domain, manifest destiny, slave-holding, low-wage-paying, advantage-taking, murdering, homesteading. Let's not forget the usurpation of resources, culture, promise for the future. Abusers are born of taking of tangibles, taking of intangibles. Abusers are born of traditions of apartheid, shoo-in job opportunities, economic exclusion, the presumed right to know-what's-best-for-everybody-and-plan-without-input.

For those of us whose parents were still able to shield us, to hide us in unwanted corners, yet unrecognized pockets of resources, these things were hard to know, hard to see, hard to interpret as something to run away from. Take education, you know, public education, the kind you impose by law. The kind that is separate. The kind that is as likely to be ameliorated by *Brown v. Board of Education* as the *Exxon Valdez* oil spill is likely to be cleaned up by Exxon Mobil. That kind. The deliberately stingy kind. We didn't see it comin'. Thought we were doing the right thing by educating ourselves. Didn't know that a public education at the hands of all-white educators would become a risk factor for suicide, the rate increasing with every year of exposure to the culture-robbing elements of the public education tsunami/blizzard/earthquake/drought.

When you grow up thinking that you are all right just the way you are, all-white-administered public education doesn't just hit you full-face and knock you down. It hits you square in the teeth and leaves your lips numb. And every time you recover and try to lift your face to speak, you are struck full-force again, until your knees are ragged from the fall, and your forearms are welted from the blows intended to make you expose your beautiful face, and you learn to hide the possibly exposed bits of your downturned face behind your dangling hair, and you neither move nor speak until you think your abuser desires you present to abuse at whim and defecate on at will. That is what happens. You don't know what's coming. You have no cultural upbringing, no sensible multigenerational preparation for this. You are told that the boarding school days were bad and are over and that this will be better. And you believe it. Because the boarding schools killed the man, even though they could not touch the Indian. And America claims that it knows better now, and it will fix the Indians.

But not itself. America would not dare fix itself. That's where educating the Indian comes in. It's about educating the Indian to stay in place, on the bottom, just as it was taught in the boarding schools. Just ask Ogitchidaakwe. No, that's OK. You sit back. Put your feet up. Relax. I'll tell you about Ogitchidaakwe. You don't have to come looking for her. You don't have to work hard. You don't have to put in any overtime. You don't have to think. You don't have to try to do your job. Just sit back. Relax. The story of Ogitchidaakwe will come to you. You don't even have to read this. You can just turn on your TV, close your eyes, maybe try to read something else. Ogitchidaakwe will just come sneaking up and read herself to you. She will curl around your morning coffee cup like a wisp of smoke, like steam from tea, like heat rising from the rim to your lips.

She was a warrior. Shhhh. . . . You're not supposed to know that. It's a cultural secret. And I'm only letting you know so that you will be one of the few, the special, the ones who understand the deep, secret, mysterious meaning of the Women's Warrior Society. Shhhh!!! Don't say it out loud. We don't want people to know that it still exists. We don't want people to know that you believe in these things. This could be construed as a stereotype, you know, this warrior thing. It might interfere with that whole Indian-culture-is-dead-dysfunctional-and-washed-up thing that we've got to keep on the surface, if we're really going to educate those Indians to meet our needs. So best keep it under your hat, under your belt, in your pants, that whole warrior thing. Better just sleep with it. Take it home and caress it at night, sneak in and unbutton its blouse, feel yourself burn and engorge with the knowledge of its existence. But best keep it a secret. Your secret. A secret that makes you better than everybody else. A secret that gives you power. Indian culture is dead and dysfunctional, washed up, doesn't need that power and that knowledge any more. Best lure that idea into your own personal bag of good stuff, take it out when you need it; maybe get a good book out of it. Maybe get a high-paying job at a college or university, lecture to the ignorant, show them how smart you are, how you know more about those Indians than those Indians know about themselves.

Sit back, relax. Ogitchidaakwe got a story or two to tell. She gonna act them out for you. Dress up like an Indian for you. Appear whenever you need a good Indian story to tell at whim, whenever you need to be better than a dumb ol' Indian, one you can defecate on at will, just so everybody around you knows who's boss. Impress your friends. Be a shaman. Be the next Joseph Campbell. Henry Rowe Schoolcraft and William McKinley aren't done yet. The homesteaders, the fur traders, the churches, the lumber barons, the cattle ranchers, the business elite, the military industrial barons, they are not done yet. The all-white teachers, the all-white authors of children's books, the all-white judges and juries and probation officers are not done yet. There's just enough room for one more usurper-of-Indian-land-base-and-culture-and-tradition-and-job-opportunities-and-casino-moneys to move into this neighborhood and squeeze out just a little bit more. So you, you put your feet up, sit back, listen. . . . You don't have to work hard for these stories. These stories gonna come to you. 'Cause you're special. Lived the benefits of privilege all your life. Need to maintain that status quo. Need things to come to you easy, just for showing up. That's the way it works.

OK. Don't worry. You showed up. Now a couple of these stories gonna wrap themselves around you. Let you take them home with you. Maybe be real nice and let you think it was your own idea. Start at your ankle, wrap themselves around your calf, slide up your thigh at night, whisper in your ear. Sneaky stories, them stories. Waitin' for someone special, just like you.

OGITCHIDAAKWE

She didn't know what was coming. She was naïve. She was young and *beautiful* and naïve. She had elk and windstorms and wild mustangs and '57 Chevys running in her hair. She had long, wide eyes that whispered of secrets and turned away with white-smiled giggles and girlishness in a defiant and untamable way. The white boys called her "exotic," and the Indian mothers called her "loved one," and the white teachers called her "trouble." And she blew in and out of the safety of her Indian world and the hazards of the non-Indian world like a tickleweed along the highway, smiling that smile, flashing those eyes, turning that head full of elk and windstorms, wild horses and beautiful, shining, lustful things. And she was naïve. She did not know that she did all of these things.

Her mother had told her that she had wild, running animals in her hair. But, where she came from, so did everyone else. Her grandmother told her that the sun rose in her eyes. But, where she came from, this was a common thing. Her aunties told her that wild dogs sang to her at night and that they wanted to feel the caress of her hand, would domesticate themselves for the scent of her sweet breath in the night. But they had told this to her sisters as well. They had, in fact, been told these very things themselves, those mothers, those grandmothers, those aunties. They had no other reality to share, other than their own beauty, and they held themselves up to those young women like mirrors, beautiful, steady, ageless mirrors of motherhood and love and hard work and expectations.

So she didn't know what was coming.

Shhhhh. . . . It's cultural. It's special. It's a secret. You are not supposed to know about these things. You know the stuff you saw in the movies? It's sort of like that, but not so simple. We'd never let the real thing get out and be used in the movies. It's like that with secret societies. We save the real version for people like you, yeah, 'cause you're special. We always been lookin' for a friend like you, one we can trust, one who can really understand what it's like to be spiritual like one of us, one who knows the truths behind the deepest secrets, one who is the *real* Indian inside, the one who has the heart of a buffalo, the eyes of an eagle, the ears of the sensitive deer, the sniffing ability of the wisest of the trickster coyotes and the mysterious wolves, the palate of a cultural connoisseur, the touch of a tender, overseeing parent, of a guardian, of a lover, of a swiiindler.

Yeah, you. You. . . . Pssssst. . . . Got some secrets to tell ya. Just you, nobody else. Keep this secret. Don't tell nobody. Swear ya won't tell nobody, an' I'll tell ya all about da *sweatlodge*. Yeah, da *sweatlodge*. Really. You'll be the only other person alive besides us who knows about it, I mean *really* knows about it, like someone we can really trust, one who can really understand what it's like to be spiritual like one of us, one who knows the truths behind the deepest secrets, one who is the *real* Indian inside, the one who has the heart of a buffalo, the eyes of an eagle, the ears of the sensitive deer, the sniffing ability of the wisest of the trickster coyotes and the mysterious wolves, the palate of a cultural connoisseur, the touch of a tender, overseeing parent, of a guardian, of a lover, of a swiiindler.

Yeah, really. I'm gonna tell you all those things. And then I'm gonna tell you about da secret society. Yeah, I know, you didn't think that the women had a secret society. You didn't read about it in Anthropology 101.

It's that secret. No shit, really, I mean it's *that* secret. We been foolin' y'all all these years. You didn't even know about it, didn't know how we kept our culture alive all those years, in our living rooms, in our woodlots, in our sheds, on distant beaches and islands, in desert crevices, on snowy bluffs, in our hearts. You didn't read about it in Anthropology 101.

And thanks to every textbook and piece of children's literature and local museum exhibition and local newspaper you ever read, you think that our culture is currently dead, due to the excellent job your ancestors and predecessors did at exterminating and improving us (in spite of our limited ability). Oh, yeah, and you didn't read about it in Anthropology 101. 'Cause the guys who wrote the textbooks read the same books and exhibitions and cultural concepts that you did. You know, the ones that said we were cute, primitive, and so incredibly simple that one could learn how to be us by merely reading a book or two in Anthropology 101 or a novel or two that spoke of simple and needy Indian folk who needed superior, supervisory cultures and sensitive individuals to show us how to take care of ourselves after you took away everything we ever had. Took away our inheritance, then told us to start life from scratch, like you, even though you had an inheritance. Took away our social status, special connections, preference in the job market, then told us to start life from scratch, like you, even though you had social status, special connections, preference in the job market. Took away our rights to see ourselves as anything but underlings who exist merely to serve you, even though you see yourselves as superior, as able to be guardians and decision makers for us, as one of many we can trust, one who can really understand what it's like to be spiritual like one of us, one who knows the truths behind the deepest secrets, one who is the *real* Indian inside, the one who has the heart of a buffalo, the eyes of an eagle, the ears of the sensitive deer, the sniffing ability of the wisest of the trickster coyotes and the mysterious wolves, the palate of a cultural connoisseur, the touch of a tender, overseeing parent, of a guardian, of a lover, of a swiiindler.

Yeah, come on over here. I'm gonna teach you 'bout da wimen's warrior society. Tough wimen, dem wimen. Got long, beautiful hair, dem wimen. Got elk and windstorms and wild mustangs and '57 Chevys running in their hair. They got long, wide eyes that whisper of secrets and turn away with white-smiled giggles and girlishness in a defiant and untamable way. But don't tell nobody. It's a secret.

THEY ARE SHAPE SHIFTERS

They reinvent themselves constantly, those women warriors. They are like she-wolves.

Ogitchidaakwe, she started out one thing, became another. Did it like the turn of a leaf in a breeze. Did it that effortlessly, really. Because she must have been a liar or none of those things. No one could be all the things that Ogitchidaakwe had become. She became an earnest student, looking in the right direction all the time, walking away from Indianness all the time, being quiet and docile all the time. She became a scholarship student, studying all the time, washing dishes in the dormitories all the time, cleaning houses for the faculty members all the time, while she learned five new languages, passed the proficiency exams, learned the important stuff about Anglo-Euro-American culture and a little bit about African Americana, too. But not the Indians, not the Indians like her. Learned about the cool people, the !Kung Bushmen. The long-extinct Timvqva and Calusa. The docile Navajo. The exotic Sioux. The Bedouin tribesmen. The history of the British. The history of the Italians. The art of the Renaissance. The age of Romanticism. The golden days of exploration and colonization. Learned to sing about Christopher Columbus. Learned it all. Got about as liberally educated as one could get. Learned about all those peoples. The cool ones. But maybe not her kind. Her kind was not exotic. Her kind was not cool. Her kind was not worthy of study.

So she learned all of that stuff. And then she found out that she still wasn't good enough. So she got herself a master's degree in stuff. But she still wasn't good enough. So she got a doctorate in stuff. But she still wasn't good enough. And somebody said, become a teacher, because you Indians, you really need teachers. And somebody else said, become a nurse, because you Indians, you really need nurses. And somebody else said, become a dealer in the casino, because you Indians, you really need dealers in the casinos. Ph.D. in second-hand cigarette smoke. Postdoctoral work in unskilled labor.

Nobody said, "We need you."

But they did need her. They needed her to teach to. They needed her to fill their classrooms of nothingness. They needed her to be lesser, to dictate to, to "acculturize," to acclimate, to accentuate the superiority of themselves. And they taught her well, what they wanted her to be. And, damn, did she learn well, what they wanted her to be. She did it so well that they got angry and they changed the rules. Said, sorry, not good enough . . . better-than-us not good enough, bad timing, we don't need that no more, be something else, you really fucked up becoming the best teacher, we don't need no teachers no more, you really fucked up becoming the best nurse, we don't need no nurses no more, you really fucked up becoming the best nuclear physicist, the best surveyor, the best artist, the best lecturer, the best public servant, we don't need them things no more. Just need casino dealers and toilet-bowl scrubbers and dishwashers in the dormitories. What's wrong with you, think you gonna be something bigger than that?

We need you to be docile. So that Ogitchidaakwe, she becomes docile. Becomes the best docile she knows how. Looks around her for docile. Imitates that docile. Does docile so good she becomes a caricature of docile. White man says, "You actin' all docile like that tryin' to make fun of me? You actin' all docile like that tryin' to draw attention to yourself? Tryin' to make me look like the bad guy told you to be all docile?" And that Ogitchidaakwe, she says no sir and looks down at her feet.

He kicks her off the sidewalk this way and that. She looks at her toes, says, maybe I better not be so docile. That's right, that white man says, be like me. Act like me. Talk down to people. Be demanding to people. Let people know you better than them. And that Ogitchidaakwe, she tries that just a little bit, sees nobody likes that, looks around for something else to try on.

That Ogitchidaakwe, she says, well maybe being smart didn't work so good, better be dumb. And that Ogitchidaakwe, she looks around, looks at all the good examples of dumb she can find, and she pretends to be dumb. And she does one hellacious job of being dumb. Does dumb so good, nobody dummer. Does dumb so good, white folks start sayin', "You so dumb, you work for me for free, I let you live in my shed, let you glean my fields, let you get two, three, maybe six or seven part-time, seasonal jobs, just made for dumb people like you. Supposed to be poor, people like you. Lucky for everything we toss your way, people like you."

That Ogitchidaakwe, she works for free, just to keep a roof over her head, shelter her from the cold most of the time, keep her fed just enough to survive. Never save. Never plan for more. That Ogitchidaakwe, she starts to think that maybe because she's so good at being dumb and poor, maybe she could have a raise, and those white folks hiring her for free or next to nothing, they get pretty darned angry, that Indian woman wants to change the status quo, say, what's the matter with you? And that Ogitchidaakwe, she starts to think that maybe dumb and poor is not so good. She watches those white folks—say, we own this, we own that, we earn more than you, that makes us better than you.

So she decides that maybe she'd better be a scholar, that Ogitchidaakwe. She decides that maybe she'd better have bloodlines, be erudite, hold her head up, be equal. But those white neighbors, they don't like that much, and they tell that Ogitchidaakwe that she's got no business thinking those things about herself. She's just an Indian. Supposed to be lesser. Supposed to be the reason for her own lack of success. Supposed to apologize for herself before she even leaves the womb.

So that Ogitchidaakwe, she decides that maybe she better not be a person, maybe better be something bigger. Maybe be a spirit. Maybe be a whirlwind. Maybe be a wolf. Maybe be a bear, a fish, a snake, maybe just an idea floating on a soft breeze, a spider in the woodpile. And that Ogitchidaakwe, she keeps reinventing herself. She studies that woodpile, figures out when that woodpile needs a spider. Becomes that spider. She studies the leaves in the trees, figures out the most beneficial time to be a persistent wind. She studies the waters, decides when to be a big fish, a small fish, a darting fish, an invisible fish. She studies her environment, looks for opportunity, and changes at will. They all do that, those women warriors.

Those women warriors, they know when to be lovers, when to be haters, when to be friends, foes, smooth, soft, hard and dangerous. Those women warriors, they know how to use a grain of sand as a weapon. They can fight you back with your own voice, your own words, your own angry breath. They can climb in and out of your expectations and crawl out of your whims on their hands and knees if necessary. They train in secret camps, in sheds and cornfields and forest glens, under the heavy branches of snow-loaded spruce, at kitchen tables, and at computers in public libraries. They cannot be destroyed. Every time one of them is murdered, she reincarnates, becomes new and young flesh, with flashing eyes and elk and windstorms and wild mustangs and '57 Chevys in her hair.

THE SWEATLODGE

OK, these three Indians walk into a bar. . . . No, wait a minute. That's an inaccurate stereotype.

OK, these three Indian women warriors walk into the convenience store-slash-gas station halfway between the casino, where the jobs don't pay too well, and the tribal library, where the jobs pay even worse. . . . And this one warrior says to the other one, "I was processing your paperwork over at the governmental center [the portable building next to the trailer that holds the library], and I couldn't help but wonder, since you're tutoring her kids, will you tutor mine."

And the one warrior says to the other warrior that she's only doing it as a favor for the third warrior, and it doesn't even pay enough to cover the gas and the hassle of putting away other projects to drive fifty miles in the dead of winter. And the first warrior says, "Yeah, but I just want you to help my daughter with her senior project up at North Arbor School."

And the second warrior, she says she doesn't mind doing that, since the kid's so darned close to escaping the system. But she doesn't want to set foot in that school. Racist institutions, those schools. Still has a visceral response to those buildings and those people in them, she says. And those first two warriors, they figure out a workable schedule for meeting in a public library that's closer to where they live, and the white ladies that run it are pretty mellow about letting the Indians in. And that third warrior lady doesn't even have much to say about it, except that she's glad she got a tutor for her kids.

And those Indian ladies pay for their gas and potato chips and they ride home in their old, cheap cars, and they put in maybe the last quarter shift on their fourteen-hour days.

OK, these two Indian women warriors walk into a bar. . . . Boy, you just can't get past those stereotypes, can you?

These two women warriors walk into a small-town public library. They are among a half dozen or so Indians who have dared to set foot in a public facility in this all-white town in oh, maybe a hundred years. (Except for the jail and the courthouse, and, rarely, the grocery store, but not usually.) While the middle-aged one is waiting for the young one, she flips through the only "Indian" book in the library. It is a picture book of powwow dancers. The dancers are all from different tribes, dressed up in their regalia and holding eagle feathers. The captions under the photos are mostly about spirituality. And they all have "special" names in quotation marks, so they're called stuff like

Bud "Laughing Horse" Smith
Harold "Eagle Catcher" Szyzkowski
Tiffany "Earth Mother" Shagonabe
Leslie "Highfoot" Loonfeather
Richard "Lightning Eye" Dark Horse
Elizabeth "Hearth Woman" Fanning
Jeremy "Broken Arrow" Wilson
Anthony Albert "End of the Trail" Jefferson III
Roberto "Wild Eye" Todacheenee
Beverly "Corn Woman" Lucero
June "Quick to Paint" Jordan
Joy "Kokopelli Doll" Harjo
Maria "Tax-Free Cigarettes" Campbell
Drew "Hayden" Taylor
Lois "Buffalo Chip" Beardslee
Lori "Archaeological Relic" James
Heidi "Anthropological Artifact" Raphael

Arlo "Feathered Headdress Made from Chickens" Eichstadt
Marie "Can You Make That Buckskin Dress a Little Shorter" Knake

And then that young warrior, she comes into da public library. And that middle-aged one, she says, "You don't wanna see this. Excuse me a minute." And she puts that powwow book back on its shelf with the other six social studies/world cultures books. Then she wipes her hands on the armpits of her winter coat, hoping maybe to make that ickiness come off her hands before she sits in close and lovingly with the young warrior and guides her through her initiation.

Now, this young warrior, she's got to do a project for senior-class project-presentation day in the school library. And she's got to pass her senior project, or she's not going to get her high school diploma, no matter how good her grade point average is. And she picked powwows for her subject matter, and she's comparing the for-the-public commercial powwows with the smaller, traditional powwows, because she likes the smaller, more traditional powwows best; and so does that older warrior.

But that middle-aged warrior, she's been around the block, been in and out of the public schools as student and parent and unwanted Indian, been to college and back, been to academia and public institutions and back, and she doesn't want to see this poor girl have to lick her wounds too badly. Because she understands why the girl chose powwows for her subject matter. She understands why the girl needs that traditional culture to keep herself grounded within the dense atmosphere of racism in the all-white-staffed schools with their all-white-written textbooks and their field trips to the all-white-conceived museum exhibits. She also knows that the Indian subject matter would soil the psyches of those all-white committee members. She knows that that girl's senior project will have to be outstanding.

So they sit together at that computer, in a small corner of the library, and the nice white lady volunteer there is only abusive to them twice. And those Indian women warriors, they smile up from that computer, flash the whites of their long eyes, and adjust the barrettes that hold their long hair up in tight buns so as to prevent the elk and windstorms and wild mustangs and '57 Chevys that reside in their tresses from running loose and knocking the long rows of sacrosanct white books from their solid footing within the community and its power structure. And it is there, in that space that they temporarily make their own, that those two warriors refine that already-fine written report, shuffle paragraphs, insert commas, and adjust the sentence structure to make the whole thing sound more white in the hopes that they might teach those white teachers something and make it just a little bit easier for the next woman warrior who comes along.

"It's not that I don't love our dialect," the elder warrior explains. "Our dialect is beautiful." And the young one looks back in confusion. "Dialect?" "Yes, you know, we have one, the way we talk when we are with each other and family and we are comfortable, and it spills out of us and wraps itself around us and makes us feel good. That is a dialect, a beautiful, beautiful, meaningful dialect. And we need to take it out of this paper before you turn it in, so that they look at it in a different light instead of just an Indian paper, and you have to understand that it is not you, it is not us, it is them. They are stupid. They are scary. The college programs with the lowest entry requirements are educational administration, followed by elementary education, followed by, yeah, you get it, so don't take it personally, it's not you, it's not us, it is them."

And these things are whispered in the sweatlodge of public brick and wood siding and glass-windows-that-look-out-at-the-river and the historic files of the local weekly newspaper that says terrible things about the Indians. And their beautiful warrior faces shine in the dim glow of the computer monitor as Microsoft Word preserves their wisdom and sentiments on a small disk that will be removed from that building and its sensibilities when the women glide out that library door, following the running elk and windstorms and wild mustangs and '57 Chevys that have blown loose from their constrained tresses. The warriors have gazed intently upon the embers of their passion and will to succeed in that small clockless room that they have not noticed that the library is closing; and the white volunteer who is normally so nice insists on scolding them; but her voice only rides away on the breeze and the elk as the warriors smile sideways through the long corners of those wide eyes and lope to distant trucks and spiritual mounts and hear only one another's voices reassuring each of them of their own competence and beauty, as relentless and undeniable as the elk and windstorms and wild mustangs and '57 Chevys that run through their hair.

WIMEN WARRIORS ARE SNEAKY

They're so good at outdoing their masters, those wimen warriors. Really. You gotta watch 'em. Sneaky. Think you got 'em beat, on accounta they're weaker'n you. You been lookin' 'round, lookin', lookin' fer some minority woman to take advantage of, worth less than you, don't ya know. . . . Worked yer way through wimen. Tried white women. You got a little too firm, they turned you away. Tried a pregnant girl once. I guess even she wasn't desperate enough, had other options, parents with money. Hell, I even marched in Selma, Alabama, but those black girls still wouldn't sleep with me. Tried a Mexican girl. But, jeez, she had family. So, finally, there's this Indian girl. Hell, them Indians, a whole bunch of 'em got no goddam family. Family been killed off—they blame it on unemployment, suicide, liquor, no health insurance. . . . Sheesh, you name it, those Indians claim they die from it.

Whole lotta those Indian wimen got nobody. You give 'em just a little bit, just a little bit, maybe take them out for a burrito, give 'em a ride or two in your car, them Indians, they fall into your arms. Think you were the greatest thing since canned peaches.

I had one of 'em once. Took a lot of work. 'Cause you know, she thought she was just as good as me. But I showed her. I crawled under that stupid little Chevy of hers, and I unscrewed the drain plug on her oil reservoir. Oil ran out of her, out onto that two-lane highway out there in the mountains. So she hitchhiked back to the village, found me, or maybe she ran, ran like a wild dog through the hills, up the arroyos. She could have done that, you know. She never even left any footprints when she walked, said the wind steals away footprints in the desert.

She asked me to help her tow that dead Chevy's body home that day.

Borrowed a rope already. Had a rope wrapped around her shoulders. Looked sexy as shit. Looked like she thought that she was something special, maybe better than me, maybe didn't need somebody like me, except to tow that old Chevy home. But she needed me. It was me . . . or hitchhike — and I made sure she was too fucking scared to hitchhike, even too fucking scared to run through those hills like a wolf or a coyoteee.

DAT WIND

The rainy season would be starting soon. She'd been talking to Eunice about it a few nights before. "There's a ring around the moon," she said. Dat wind gonna bring dem clouds, soon.

Moisture. Sustenance. Rainfall.

Nice wind comes along. Brings dem clouds over da mountaintops, dat wind. Brings irrigating rains, dat wind. Better tie up dat wind, before it gets too strong. Be as strong as a wind, like her mother, like her grand-mothers. Put up with anything to survive. Strong like dat wind, you gotta be, where she comes from. Important, dat wind. They take care of each other, dem warriors an' dat wind.

This one, she came on an easterly breeze.

This one, she came with the north winds tucked into the pocket of her parka.

This one, she comes periodically with constant zephyrs from the west.

And that one, she crept northward, arid and hot-blooded, with moisture from the Gulf of Mexico balled up in her fists.

They've been sitting together around a tin shepherd's stove now, letting that heat pull the exhaustion from their bones. Letting that wind pull the borrowed calories from those chunks of firewood. Letting that wind pull the strain of unskilled labor up the stovepipe. Sharing the piñon nuts they'd stuffed into their pockets from the ridges above the arroyo after a long day of hard work. They were sweet and greenish, dark like coffee beans, those nuts. Could have just as easily been beechnuts. . . . First came a frost to loosen the stems. Then came the wind, that wind that knocked them down where the young women warriors could reach them.

Just enough rain here to sustain them . . . the trees, the nuts, the company of warriors.

Today she'll bring her bags of onions in from the shed, so they won't freeze. Yesterday Eunice slid her pumpkins into the sun, to sweeten their flesh.

"Save me some of those seeds." (Moisture. Sustenance. Opportunity.)

Cheryl found an outdated case of tofu in a dumpster in Albuquerque. They carried a bucket of water up from Elio's well to rinse it. Iris brought home a box of slices from the outside of the zucchini from that restaurant where she fries the appetizers every night. Those slices are threaded and drying in pale green crinkles in every house in the village.

"We used to smoke the fish dry back home, pound it into a powder." Too wet to dry food in the sun back home, but cold enough to keep it, once smoked. Don't matter if your grannies was Anasazi or Anishinaabe . . . know how to make somethin' out of nothin'. Don't matter if it's from da woods or da lakes or them dumpsters in da city.

Moisture. Sustenance. Full bellies.

Dere's a nice wind now. Knock some more wild nuts out of dem trees, dat wind. Fill up da springs, dat wind. Bring a good blanket of snow, dat wind. Make a good excuse to light da woodstoves, dat wind.

"Who is driving to the university tomorrow?"

Is dat Subaru running?
Sort of.

Is dat pickup truck running?

Maybe not so steady this week.

"Better take dat ol' Chevy."

WIMEN WARRIORS ARE NOT BORN, THEY ARE MADE

Don't know who those fucking, goddam Indians are, think they're something special. Think they've got a different culture. Think they're better
than me. Tried dating another Indian bitch before, this bitch Alberta,
fuckin' Zuni. But she ran back to her fuckin' alcoholic, piece-of-shit Zuni
family, had her worthless, drunk Zuni brother stick his worthless empty
fist under my chin, tell me to leave his whore sister alone. But he didn't
scare me. I grew up in New York City. Nothin' fuckin' scares me. My great-
grandparents were immigrants. They homesteaded. Made something out
of that land in upstate New York that the Indians couldn't even hold on
to. *They* were tough. Indians think they know tough. *I'm* tough. I wasn't
scared by that Zuni, even though he called me a short fuckin' Jew. Yeah,
I walked away. But not really. He just *thinks* I walked away. I know how to
take my time. I know how to get even. I got an Indian bitch to marry me
anyhow. *I'm* the boss now. Wave a fist under my chin and tell me to leave
your wimen alone now.

They're supposed to be *special*, you know—quiet and docile—not
talking back like that. They're not real Indians, you know, the ones that
talk back and drink and get mean like that. They might look like Indians,
but they're not supposed to be like that. They're supposed to be gentle.

I studied psychology in graduate school. And I put in my time with
them. Did counseling with those Indians. Did rehab with 'em. This one
kid, a quadriplegic, lived in the Indian hospital in Albuquerque. His family would all drive out to see him once a month from out on that Navajo
reservation way the hell over on the other side of the state. And they'd get
drunk as shit, that family. And there was that kid, couldn't go anywhere,
couldn't get off those machines in that hospital, and all he had were a

bunch of drunken fuckin' Indians come to see him first weekend of every month. Shit. What a shitty life. What a shitty family. All of 'em pilin' into the back of a pickup truck, like it was a goddam convertible. You ever hear the term "Navajo convertible"? That's what the locals call it, when they see a truckload of 'em goin' down the highway. Stickin' their heads out in the breeze like a bunch of dogs.

I knew about those Navajos. They needed me. Needed me to tell them to stay fucking sober, so they could face up to what they probably did to their own kid. They probably got into an accident driving drunk. They needed people with degrees in psychology, like me, to counsel them in substance abuse. They needed me to counsel their kids—to teach them how to get jobs, so they'd quit being so lazy, treating that reservation like an excuse. Hell, I even ran a special education class training them how to pass the entrance exams for the armed services. Because they couldn't even do that—especially the ones with the low IQs—so I worked with those military recruiters, to make sure that even the dumb ones could pass the entrance exams. They were mostly Mexicans and Indians, you know, the kids in special education. ROTC was one of the only optional classes they could take. My bosses thanked me for meeting their needs.

You know, even if people don't know how ignorant and unsophisticated they are, you can straighten them out. You can trick them, tell them anything, and they don't act like they suspect anything. Don't even know you're persuading them. That's why I like living here in New Mexico. It's like shooting fish in a barrel. They need me.

WARM WIND

They are fingering one another's barrettes, admiring the beads, the quills, the turquoise, the ancient shells, the polished bits of bone and solid ancient trees. They relax their workloads for a piece of a day, relax their mentalities, relax their constraints, relax the clasps on the elk and windstorms and wild mustangs and '57 Chevys that run through their hair. . . .

There's a warm wind. Where will it blow them today?

"Let's go up into the Sandias to find some wild raspberries."

"Let's go up to the Jemez and dig for bear root. We can soak in the hot springs on the way back."

"Let's go down to Torreon and pick wild mint and *estafiate*. We can watch the hippies try to speak Spanish at the general store on the way back." (Watch them live a rural, low-income fantasy between the ease of affluent childhoods and the comfort of white-privileged employment once they become ready for it.)

"Let's go up the canyon behind the artesian well in Yrisarra and look for *verdolagas* and pictographs." The old people, they ate the verdolagas, too, when they came to paint those canyon walls.

"I found some old pottery shards up there with the old people's finger-prints fired in the clay. My mom used to find those, too, back home. She'd grind them up for her pots." Put the old people in your pots. Maybe put a tight lid on them pots. Store some warm breezes in those pots. Maybe make a real big pot. Keep a windstorm in a pot like that. Climb into a pot like that and hide. Hide from angry words. Hide from unemployment. Hide from hard times.

"Let's go find some clay and make some pictographs." Put your finger-prints on those canyon walls for your kids to find.

"You think we'll ever get married and have kids?"

"Maybe be mothers."

"Maybe be grandmothers."

"Maybe be aunties."

"Maybe be doctors."

"Maybe be lawyers."

"Maybe be governors."

"Maybe fight hunger."

"Maybe build bridges."

"Nice barrette."

"Thanks. I made it."

Big barrette. You could keep a windstorm in a nice barrette like that.

"Let's go visit my brother in the hospital. Then we can go over to Wither-spoon. I hear people turn their horses loose there when they can't afford to feed them any more."

"Better take the Chevy."

ONLY A WARRIOR...

She doesn't remember the name of the lake.

She only remembers its convolutions.

She remembers how the day started out gray, cold, overcast.

It might have been misty.

It might have been so misty that you couldn't see twenty feet ahead,

And then, when you least expected it, there was a sharp turn.

From the back of the canoe, her mother would say, "Just keep paddling. I know this lake."

And this sense of the unknown, it took her back

To the long car ride, only a few small toys, only one precious book, the old dog in her own small cubby on the floor on one side in the back seat.

The full Toyota humming smoothly and reliably through the states she'd seen on a map, while she was drowsy, excited, frightened.

"Paddle hard left." The voice was sure and steady from the mist in the back of the canoe.

She remembered that the air was warm and moist when they stopped to sleep sitting up somewhere on the Oklahoma Turnpike.

It had been the first time she had felt warmth for a long time.

"Do you feel the moisture on your face?" her mother asked. "It's a gift. I haven't felt that moisture for a long time."

The sun wanted to break through the fog, but it was too dense.

"You see that word? It says 'Chicago.' You tell me every time you see the word 'Chicago.' You point."

The turn is so abrupt, her paddle scrapes on sand and pebbles.

"You're a good reader. I'm proud of you. You're a good reader."

Nothing ahead but another long bay. "Where are we?"

"St. Louis."

Seventeen lanes of traffic; she counted them.

"We're crossing the Mississippi River."

Nothing but cornfields and quiet on the other side. Flat, open, safe.

The sun broke through in the next basin.

"Do you hear that? Do you hear that?" Red-winged blackbird, chipping sparrow, old crow, comfort, security, sunrise, consistency, tomorrows.

"That's a nice point, up ahead there."

In the sunshine.

"If I was an eagle, I'd sit in that big pine tree on that point. And I'd look for my next meal." Sustenance. Comfort. Tomorrows.

She remembers that tree, when she closes her eyes.

She remembers the warmth of the sunshine and visibility through clear water.

Small, comforting pebbles and the ripples of her own paddle in the calm.

"Back paddle on the right." Confidence and assurance from the steering end of the canoe.

She remembers the scrape of the canoe on sand.

She remembers the comfort of solid ground.

She remembers the freedom of standing up, stretching her legs, spreading her arms, singing. . . .

"Do you smell that? Do you smell that?"

Damp, fishy. "A big bird like that, it can teach you where the fish are."
Independence.

She remembers the white streams at the base of the tall, straight tree.

"It's a gift."

It's eagle poop, Mom.

Good things can come in foul packages. Strength. Free will.

"Look," she says, "it's been eating crayfish."

"And mice." Biology lessons with a poking stick.

She remembers how she saw the long white tail feather first, before her mother; and she reached for it.

But her mother held her hand back momentarily. "You need to understand something. . . .

"Only a warrior can pick up an eagle feather."

But what about me?

"Go ahead. That's your feather. You earned it."

THE CASTE SYSTEM

Someone needs to tell her story.

She has been so disenfranchised, so excluded from the mainstream and the norms and the expectations of American society that she is too far below the reach of helping arms. There are no institutions that recognize, process, or serve her needs. Even the lowest paid of the public servants are so much better off than she that they cannot fathom her difficulties. Even sympathy is out of her reach, because, other than being light brown, she appears to be normal and healthy and capable of attaining the American dream. There appears to be no reason why she cannot overcome all of her obstacles and become something greater than dictated by her birth into an unacknowledged caste system.

Yet she lives so far down on the bottom, she has fallen so far between the cracks, that she can reach up only to those who abuse and exploit those on the bottom. So, for every hour of labor she spends, she benefits, on average, by only minutes. She has no cultural capital, no social capital, no capital in the form of sympathy or compassion or cultural awareness of human resources as valuable resources.

And she is tired.

She was once a beautiful child. And loved, if only briefly. She lost her parents—perhaps to domestic violence, perhaps to socioeconomic inequality, perhaps to racism, perhaps to random gunfire, perhaps to inequitable military recruitment, poor distribution of assets, disease, car accident, industrial accident, boarding school, fatigue—it doesn't matter why or how she lost the one thing that all children should be born into. But that love, that acceptance and assurance of one's own place in the world, she did not have that for more than a few hours or a few days.

And no one told her that it was not her own fault.

So she went through life looking for approval. And never finding approval. And trying at every opportunity for limited approval and the limited success that was tossed her way carelessly by the gatekeepers of opportunity. She wore those risky chances like an oversized winter jacket—dove in head first, tucked her arms into the oversized sleeves, tried to stick her fingers out far enough to work productively, tried to lift her head up for fresh air from within the stale, used wraps of limited opportunity.

She saw men succeeding far more than women. So she gave in to men. But they were not men of kindness. They were not men of substantial assets. Because men of substantial assets did not look down between the cracks to find women without dowries; they looked only within their own caste. So she worked hard to please men who looked to the bottom layers of society for people without opportunity. She found pimps and sweatshop managers and corporate farmers and people who abused their wives and girlfriends. And she worked hard, but for every hour of labor she put in, she benefited by only minutes

She tried running away.

But the people at the departments of social services told her that she had brought her circumstances upon herself, through her own poor choices, and that she deserved to be punished. And the judge who officiated over her divorce told her that she had brought her circumstances upon herself, through her own poor choices, and so she could not be bothered with. And the people at the labor bureaus told her that she had brought her circumstances upon herself, through her own poor choices, and the wages owed her were too small to justify their time and effort. So every time she tried to run away from dishonesty and abuse, this woman was told that she was insignificant and unworthy of assistance, justice, or even compassion. So she continues to work more hours for less pay than people outside of her own bottom caste. And for every hour of labor she puts in, she benefits by only minutes.

And there are only twenty-four hours in a day.

She tried turning to other people who had once been in her caste — people who, by the hard work of one person or another, coupled with good fortune, had won survival and near comfort through treaty or contract negotiations; or had married well; or had been in the right place at the right time; or had fallen out of the right womb. But most of them forgot, very quickly, how far on the bottom their own parents and grand-parents had been. Most of them forgot how equal they had all been in the eyes of gods and creators and evolution and science. Most of them for-got how unequal distribution of resources and opportunities keeps even them from moving upward, from their middle- and upper middle-class placements in the unacknowledged caste system. So they look down, for human resources to exploit, human rocks in the stream to keep their feet dry, human rungs on the ladder to climb higher than, human beings to work more hours for less pay than they themselves so that they can garner the surpluses. Plan on those surpluses. Lust after those surpluses. Tuck those surpluses into their pants like toys and erotica. Guaranteed, those resources. Status quo, those resources. Distributed according to a caste system, those resources. And people above the very bottom have been convinced that they've got a chance to move upward if they only maintain the status quo and take, take, take from those below.

And for every hour she works, she benefits by no more than a few minutes.

Sometimes not at all. And she has never been told anything other than that it is her own fault — by virtue of her birth, her malfortune, her color, her poor social skills, her absence of upbringing, her bad personality, her poor choices. As though choices bore their way through the caste system like miners of diamonds and burrowers for gold and other precious, precious things. Instead, the only opportunities that reach down through the hard clay that separates her from success are opportunities without hope, opportunities to live shorter lives, harder lives, lives without real choice. Opportunities that benefit those with more resources than she has.

And the gatekeepers of success make sure that she knows that it is her fault, just to ensure that she will choose to do nothing more than work more hours, from which she will benefit by no more than a few minutes, if at all.

I'M A GOD

The Indians around here, they're pretty insignificant. I'd seen them up here when I was on vacation as a kid. I'd seen them down in Florida when my family went there on vacation, too. I know what those Indians are like—poor and shiftless and completely devoid of skills, nothing that anybody would want in this neighborhood.

I know what they want in this neighborhood. People moved up here to have a safe and healthy community and culture. I can give them that. They all want to be *from* here, own a piece of the history of here. Even though my dad was in the army, and maybe I didn't really live anywhere, we inherited this summer cottage here. And I got to stay with my grandmother a couple of times, when my mother got scared of my father, so I know the neighborhood. It was easy to fool people into thinking that I'm really *from* here. I know what this place needs better than any of them. And it doesn't need Indians.

I worked hard to get here. I mean, Jesus, I did everything right. I went to college and I got a profession, and I spent a whole year in a classroom with those miserable, hard-to-teach, underfed city kids. I took classes and got certified as an administrator. I put in my time, and I paid my dues. And every time I tried to straighten people out, they went over my head and complained—didn't like having a white guy in charge. Felt like I was abusive, didn't understand their *culture*—as if what they lived could be construed as culture!

I showed 'em. I moved up north, into a white neighborhood. I got a principal job in one of the most desirable school districts in the whole state, right next to all that public land. I lived ten miles from Lake Michigan. And boom—here came this case, this custody case, a no-brainer between an Indian woman and a white public school administrator. It just fell into my lap. Here was my chance to show them that I was a savior. I was going to make myself into a hero, and that school board would never want to get rid of me. That Indian woman, she would be easy to deal with, especially up here next to the national park, where people have money, and they don't want needy single mothers around trashing out their school district.

I couldn't believe it. I couldn't believe it when Henrietta came in and showed me the letters from the guy. Three in one week. On official school district stationery. And two more the next week. Here was this guy, a public school administrator like me — I could tell by the letterhead — and he'd lost visitation rights to his daughter, who was brought to my school district by a runaway wife. An Indian, Jesus, I mean I took her off the substitute teacher list as soon as I found out she was an Indian and was involved in something like this.

We don't need her type — some unemployed woman who'd come to the school counselor only months before asking for help. Asking if we had a clothing bank. As *if*, as *if*! As if we even *need* a clothing bank, like they did down there in Flint, where there were all those damned minorities without jobs. Welfare mothers, slept with the wrong guy. Bunch of jungle bunnies. Bunch of Mexicans, too. All of them sleeping around and breeding like flies, not learning English, and not taking care of their kids. And now here was one of them messing around with one of *us*, one of the good guys.

This was my opportunity to make sure that women know better than to run out on their men in this neighborhood. My wife was acting out, too, back then. She was so overly sensitive, would cower and act like I was a bad guy if I said the teeniest, littlest negative thing, if I raised my voice just a little bit. Somebody just has to make sure that the women around here know who's in charge. I was going to make sure that that father got custody.

And Henrietta, the counselor, she was a big help. She was an easy mark. It was easy to recruit her to go after the Indian, because she was such a church mouse, and I know about those church mice. All I'd had to do to show my in-laws that I was a new guy who wasn't violent anymore was to become a Christian. Got reborn. Found a new, redeemed way of life. It was easy to pull that Christian bullshit on Henrietta, too, and to get her to go after the Indian. Because I was the perfect, reliable Christian guy. And it didn't hurt that Henrietta's husband used to run around on her and was paying child support to some bimbo that used to teach here. And it didn't hurt that that Indian bimbo had been a teacher, too, and was probably running around on her husband and might even jump into bed with Henrietta's husband. Henrietta was scared to death of any woman that was younger or prettier than her, likely to steal her hubby away from her—*again*. Henrietta just ate out of my hand. I'm a god. I'm a god when it comes to these things. We almost got that Indian, too. We would've, if she hadn't scared the superintendent with a lawsuit.

She still stands by me, that Henrietta, even after my wife left me, took my girls and got them to say that I hit them and scared them, when I hardly touched them at all, hardly raised my voice at all, ever. You can ask anybody. Ask the guy who was president of the school board over there in that district where those snobs next to the national park think they're better than anybody else. Even when all of those women teachers threatened the district with a sexual discrimination suit—puh-leeze, like I discriminated against those stupid women—he stood by me. We're fellow Chriiistians. . . . Welcome to the Christian club. Yup, those two are always good for a recommendation letter when the locals start to act ungrateful, no matter which school district I move to—not that I have to move around, of course. I just look upon discontent as an opportunity to move up. I still only live fifteen miles from Lake Michigan, and I'm a superintendent now, too. I'm a pretty hard guy to fire.

You know, that time when I gently touched that little bus driver, and she accidentally fell into my office wall a couple of times. . . . I told her, she was the *only* one to ever complain, just like the others. Nobody ever believes a hysterical woman over somebody like me. I learned that lesson early on with that Indian bitch.

C'mon . . . who're you gonna believe, the Indian, or the guy in the suit?

ROAD WARRIORS

Ok, these women warriors, they park in Midjin's driveway at
        seven-oh-five, and they carpool halfway across the
                county, taking turns concentrating on the slushy
snow in the wet mornings of increasing darkness
        and decreasing opportunities,

Working seasonally for seven-oh-five per hour, and overtime
        come the last week and a half before solstice and the
                happy Christmases in the happy households of the
employed and the retired, who do not work until their arms
        are numb

Packing cherry cakes, cherry cookies, cherry cocoa, cherry
        coffees, cherry nut mix, chocolate-covered cherries,
                dark chocolate—covered cherries, cherry granola,
cherry juice, cherry soda pop, cherry wine, cherry jam,
        cherry jelly, cherry preserves, cherry salad dressing,
                cherry BBQ sauce, cherry hot sauce, dried
cherries, canned cherries, frozen cherries, to bring joy
        and contentment to the seasonal visitors to cherry-
                country-formerly-Indian-country, now that the
lakes are cold and gray and the roads are slick and
        dangerous.

These women warriors, they take home the chipped and
        mislabeled jars and bags and boxes, and they store
                them between their jars and bushel baskets of

green tomatoes and potatoes, onions, wild garlic,
    blackberries, wild grape jelly, pumpkins, carrots,
        apples, self-determination, and hope,

Every morning and evening, slowly trudging along dark back
    roads, stopping at every empty intersection, looking
        both ways, because an Indian could go to jail,
rolling through an intersection like that; and they talk
    about their husbands and their kids and the white
        supervisor at the warehouse who shows up loaded a
couple of hours into their workdays and plays rock music
    he has preselected for them at a volume that makes
        their ears hurt and plays it louder to punish
them if they complain; and they are lucky to have the
    seasonal work, because an Indian can't get work around
        here, might scare the tourists in the summertime,
might offend somebody if they ask for a living wage or a
    job that matches their credentials.

Crying together in the darkness of a different car or
    pickup truck, every morning, then night, grateful when
        there's work available on Saturday, too; the
family will still be there and need them when this is all
    over; gotta make this fifteen hundred dollars last the
        next three months.

And they swap ripe orange squash and the last of their
    green tomatoes and jars of ripe tomatoes, and clothes
        that don't fit this child or that one any more,

and extra blankets now that the kids are gone, and kind
     words and hugs and jokes and favorite songs.

On Sundays, when there is daylight available to them, they
     park in Midjin's driveway at seven-oh-five, and they
       carpool halfway across the county, taking turns
concentrating on the slushy snow in the wet mornings of
     increasing darkness and decreasing opportunities.

Showing one another the places where the watercress has not
     yet been killed by the frost, where the wild grapes
       are heavy and sweetened by the frost, where old,
abandoned apple trees still yield fruit, where the grouse
     go to eat highbush tartberries, where the road comes
       too close to the cranberry bog, and little old
ladies say, "Don't you Indians know this private property
     belongs to somebody else?"

Then these women warriors, they go to late mass at Indian
     church, swapping rubber boots and blue jeans for
       church shoes and dresses-their-grandmothers-
would-approve-of, swapping desperation and underemployment
     for small donations for the less fortunate, swapping
       fear and hard labor for hopes and expectations.

And these women warriors, they will meet post-church in a
     kitchen or a shed or a barn, where they will can wild
       grape jelly, filet long whitefish from the Indian

nets, butcher legs of venison bound for stew when the time
    comes that they will have the time and leisure to
        watch stew bubble,

Then go home to fold laundry, look at homework, write out
    the bills, haul firewood, make casseroles, make love,
        make comfort, make promises, and contemplate what
they will use to pack lunches for their working husbands
    and children and themselves in the dark of the
        morning, long before they park in Midjin's
driveway at seven-oh-five and carpool halfway across the
    county, taking turns concentrating on the slushy
        snow in the wet mornings of increasing darkness and
        decreasing opportunities.

SHIT GIRL

She was ugly. But she didn't have to be. It was a matter of choice.

You see, she was not one of those women who could lie, cheat, steal, woo a man with a mere glance, a flash of beautiful, long, sideways, shooting-star eyes. She did not have that option. She was one of those women who had to get to know a man, open the door and let him know her. Because she was ugly. She didn't have to be. It was a matter of choice. Because once a person got to know her, one would have seen the beauty in her smile, the familiarity with which her eyes might crinkle in that wide, manly face. One might find a softness and an intelligence under that straight, short butch cut of graying hair, somewhere north of that nonspace where no-neck found grace and peace between a barrel chest and a square, fat-girl smile. One might have found lyricism in the deep-chested chuckle that came out of that four-foot-eight-inch solid Gumby frame.

The *ogitchidaakweyag* would've taken her in as one of their own, willingly, lovingly, wrapped their arms around her. But she rejected their every advance, pushed them away, having been erroneously taught by the insecure short men of her lineage who repeatedly abused her that anyone other than a white man was trash. It was one way they kept her demure and willing to succumb to their every whim. She slipped instead into the arms of the self-proclaimed elite, the men who abused girls in their own closets from the very cusp of their sexual development. She emulated manhood. She emulated the insecure abusive behavior of her short father who gave her short genes. And no matter how often the ogitchidaakweyag reached out and invited her to join their ranks, she repelled them, rejected them, so that the culture and presence and reality of the isolating abusers became her only world vision. She was ugly. She didn't have to be, but it was the path she chose; and perhaps her education nurtured only the angry victim in her, flinging even choice beyond her reach. Even though the og-itchidaakweyag tried to wrap elk and windstorms and wild mustangs and '57 Chevys in her short and ragged hair. She had been told, over and over, by the men who told her she was lucky to have them violating her, that such things did not exist. So she became ugly.

She wrote for the local newspaper, the ugly one. She wrote with ha-tred about the Indians. The Indians did not understand why. They knew that it could not be because she was born ugly, because the Indians did not believe that anyone could be born ugly. They knew that her ugliness was by choice. But they did not understand why she had made that choice. They would have tried to lure her out of the steel trap of abuse-induced hatred that wrapped itself around her, bound her frame into squat, asex-ual blockiness, tore her gray-brown hair into limp, short shocks. They would have told her about Zhawiigwunh, the woman who spent her ado-lescence trying to lure northward old Biboon, old Winter, whose beau-tiful white hair had become yellowed and gritty grayish by age and hard work. It was a Sisyphean task, certain times of the year. But eventually, with perseverance, she succeeded. Those ogitchidaakweyag, they wanted to tell the Ugly One about these things, to relieve her from the pressure that pushed down on her flat, square head and made her so damned short. They wanted to take her in and cradle her as one of their own. But the abuse-induced ugliness stood in front of her like a shield, kept her iso-lated from the oral traditions of the ogitchidaakweyag that had kept them resolute for thousands of years. So she fell ugly. And she got increasingly ugly as the years went on, working at an ugly, small county newspaper for her ugly boss. Having lost even the tiniest respite from ugly that youth had given her, she fell into an even uglier state.

And nothing could penetrate this ugliness. Not love by a short, fat, and insecure but kind man. Not childbirth, motherhood, neighbors and friends, community, church. Nothing, nothing could penetrate the wall of ugly that had built itself about her.

So it was from within this blocky fortress of ugly that she threw projectiles, usually hand-shaped balls of her own feces, because she was so alone and deprived of nurturing that she had nothing left to fight with. And, oddly, she kept fighting, kept resisting the abuse that had been and continued to be thrust on her by those more powerful and privileged than she. She did not know why she fought, but she did. And because she did not have access to any other reality than the reality of her abusers, she behaved with love and obedience toward her abusers; and she threw her dismal projectiles at the only creatures she had access to who she had been taught were lesser even than her. She threw her shit at the Indians.

OK, THESE WOLVES, THEY WALK INTO A LIBRARY

OK, these three Indian women warriors walk into a bar. *Shiiiistaaa!* You can still visualize that, can't you? You are so indoctrinated with that concept that it always works. You have negative-sound-bite-Indian-stereotype receptors built right into your DNA, don't you? No? What are you saying? You mean you weren't *born* ugly? It came to you? It was the result of abuse and misinformation? Then why are you still wearing that skin? Isn't it getting a little tight?

This is the way it goes: These Indian women warriors walk into the tribal library. There are more than three of them. They keep showing up. They are growing in number, and they are gravitating toward the glow of the computer-screen campfire in the farthest recesses of this modern sweatlodge. They are pacing like wild dogs that have smelled meat. They have awakened for several days in a row with no other goal than to refrain from putting guns in their mouths and pulling the triggers, having been victimized by the Ugly One. They have tossed and rolled in the rankness of alien feces for several nights in a row, and, in want of sleep, in want of rest from the assault of abuse-induced abuse, they have transformed themselves into she-wolves. Those women warriors, they have fallen back on ancient and fail-safe strategies: packlike hunting patterns, lifting their long, lean Indian noses far into the air, tilting their heads and listening like big-eared moose, feeling the air for moisture and wind and temperature, licking at paper trails and well-worn paths of racism, *shape shifting. . . .*

They are sniffing at the offal in one another's fur. They are sniffing at one another's orifices, in search of something familiar and safe, under the pungency of alien abuse. They circle the Formica-topped tables, rub against the hard plastic chairs, shed fur on the short, hard carpet. They track over the electrical cords and the multiplugged outlets, tear at the table full of military recruitment paraphernalia that is more readily available to their children upon entry to this building than even the simplest, most childlike journal or book. They back up and lower their haunches and growl at the white "teacher" who dared to trot over and salvage the recruitment "opportunity" of death brochures that America holds sacrosanct in lieu of educating her children of poverty and color. The canine teeth of the older women are slightly worn, plaque yellowed, giving them the impression of width and therefore greater strength and grasping ability. And those of the younger women are pointier, whiter, look like they could penetrate even the thickest and most foolproof excuses for continuing to push Indian children disproportionately into the military. The teacher pulls back a hand, mumbles presumed errands, and retreats through the double doors of the sweatlodge.

Those women, they curl up their lips and they bark at this retreat, guard their turf, hold firm. Their raised hackles are sprinkled with gray and with knowledge, experience, old scars, pain. They raise those lips again and snap in unison, and the February sun flees the sky, covers its ass, and makes for the nearest cloud.

They can do that, those warrior women. No shit. They can do that.

And when the room goes black, when the snow and wind and ice that they growled into the middle of their afternoons pull the plugs and kill the glow of the computer monitors and silence the whirrr of those omnipresent computer fans, those wolf women, they know what to do. They are used to this. They pad over to their stashes of candles and bottles of water, and they illuminate a table in a back corner, where they sit on hard, swooping, one-piece, cheap plastic chairs, tails tucked carefully off to the side. They stroke their damp whiskers, smooth back their hackles, lift their long Indian noses and sniff at one another just one more time, to make sure that all is safe. And the keeper of the eastern door begins to speak. "Didja see the paper?"

"Naw, I don't read it."

"I don't read it because it's not a newspaper. It's a real estate rag."

"Oh. I read it. I read it to find out what they're up to."

"I don't care what they're up to."

"I care. They scare me."

"I care. So I don't read it. It will make my blood pressure go up. It will hurt me. It is intended to hurt me."

"Hmmmm. . . ." They nod their long doggie noses in agreement.

They understand, those she-wolves. They know. They know that the Ugly One has been throwing her shit in their direction again. They look at one another. They sniff. Ah, yesss. . . . They recognize the size, the shape, the density, the texture, the color, the smell of this shit. This is familiar shit. This is the shit that the county newspaper has been throwing their way for lifetimes.

"Aaah. . . . It is the work of Those Ones."

"The Ugly Ones."

"The Throwers of Their Own Feces." Those women warriors as wolf dogs, they voice this together, with practiced precision. These are well-seasoned warriors.

WHAT REALLY GOES ON OVER AT THE TRIBAL LIBRARY

OK, these Indian women warriors walk into a tribal library. Finally, you've got it right. You visualize them now. They've put away the laundry and the housework. They've risen long before dawn, all of them. Shuffling priorities and postponing care for self. Making sure that their homes are safe and comfortable and secure. Meals for the families have been gathered and prepared. Some have been bundled away in insulating towels and tubs and set in the laps of transient children, hauled into the tribal library, stashed away next to the drinking fountain. The warriors' babies are tappy-tapping contentedly at keyboards, sliding through exercises in fractions and prime-factorization, writing essays about flatworms and gorillas and marsupial tiger wolves, playing hangman with dependent clauses and definite relative pronouns. They are munching contentedly on apples and lake trout, far from the income-generating, fructose-and-fat-laden vending machines of the public-schools-for-profit that pepper their traditional homeland like ulcers.

They slip out of their houses under the guise of mediocrity. They bundle laundry and banking and shopping lists and old canning jars full of wild mint tea into their coolers and into cardboard boxes. They top off their gas tanks, refill their travel mugs, and sharpen their pencils. They use Windex and Comet to transform the thin veneer of the metal building into safety and tradition. They howl and dig with their paws and build retaining walls and air baffles of snow and ice and tradition around that tribal library.

Then they sing. They sing high pitched and doglike. They sing quietly and demurely, like sparrows in a breeze. Then they shake their heads, rise up off their tucked-under tails and sing and yip and howl and growl themselves into a series of loud barks and howls. They bark to the right. They bark to the left. They bark up. They bark down. They bark to the east, they bark to the north, they bark to the west, they bark to the south. Good barkers, them wimen. Bark down the sun, bark up the moon, bark away the Ugly Ones, bark in new life. Helluva buncha good barkers, them wimen warriors.

Sit at that table in the back of the room. Build a fire. Sit on them haunches. Reach out dem front paws, like they was hands, warmin' 'em against that fire. Bring in hot rocks. Heat them rocks 'til they glow. Cover the windows. Lock that big glass and metal door. Maybe cover it up with an elk skin or a sheet of birch bark. Better post the clan symbols on the outside, Scotch-tape them up, so the ancestors and the wild dogs know where to find us. Bring in an old pitchfork from the barn, use it to turn those glowing hot rocks on that Formica table.

The keeper of the eastern door, she takes off her glasses and rubs them with the corner of her shirt. She is careful not to scratch them with her long, wolf-woman claws. She spreads the papers out on the table. They are contemporary stories, modern history, study after study after study after study about racism in education. They come from scholarly books. They come from scholarly journals. They come from Indians. She clears her throat, that keeper of the eastern door. She breathes in through that long doggie nose. "Didja read the paper?"

"It's not a newspaper. It's the toy of a trust-fund baby." The statement cackles out of the northern door of the sweatlodge, from the darkness, where that wolf keeper of the northern door sits on her cold haunches, hard against the snow-packed floor, not nearly well insulated enough by the short, tough carpet.

"Ahhh. . . ," those wolf women nod, "the Bean Boy."

"Ayiiih, ayiiih," those dog warriors yip, then hiss.

"Albert Van Camp, the god of Pork and Beans." It is sung from the western door as a coyotelike howling laugh.

"Seeeey-maah!" the keeper of the southern door sings out, as water and herbs and history and voices are tossed against the mere surface of those glowing volcanic rocks. The perfume and the song rise with the stone-released sulfur, and the air grows hot and thick, and each of the women warriors whispers to the other, "Keep your head down low, where the air is cooler."

They lay their heads down on the wood-patterned, smooth Formica of the cheap tables of modern educational experience, and they concentrate on the fading glow of the rocks. They blink from the heat. They feel safe for a moment, safe from the attacks on Indians that line the front pages of the flimsy substitutions for journalism that constitute the local white-flight newspaper.

"More rocks!" The woman warrior from the westernmost door hisses out.

And the auxiliary spouses and oldest sons outside the building poke open the tent flap just enough to let a few shreds of cold, blowing snow relieve the women from the intense heat. "Uh, the windchill factor out here is twenty-five below," one of them tentatively proffers.

"We are not done yet. More hot rocks!" Another pitchfork appears from the cold, and the space is eerie and glowing and stinking of sulfur and wild-dog fur and rebellion once again.

"Seeeey-maah!" the cry is released from the northern door. And the steam and herbs rise up with the sulfured air.

"Why are they doing this?" an injured voice yips from somewhere in the northwest nether regions of the rectangular conference table.

"Maybe the little god of Pork and Beans was given the finger by an Indian at an intersection." The suggestion floats on hot, sulfured air from the keeper of the western door.

"Nah. He's just a mean-spirited little jackass who hates Indians."

"But we are powerless."

"Ah, but we are here."

"I can understand why he pushes the far-right-wing pseudo-Christian business agenda in his real estate rag, with his need to protect his inheritance, but why come after us?"

"Because we are here."

"Because we are vulnerable and easy victims. Because the game of reach-out-and-hurt so easily gets out of control."

"Because we threaten his fantasies about being a tough guy in the far north; we threaten his concept of self as Indian, wild man in a plaid shirt, Paul Bunyan in designer climbing boots."

"But there's nothing here to climb."

"Just his fantasies."

"Why our children?"

"Because he wants to beat down the future generations before they have a chance to grow. He is that insecure, that desperate."

"Because the casinos make us look less vulnerable; and that makes the hapless afraid."

"Because he cannot compete against us on equal footing, and he knows that he is nothing without his father's wealth and the newspaper-as-power-tool that has been handed to him with so little effort of his own."

"Because he is insecure about the size of his dick, yip yip yip."

"Woof, woof! Heh, heh, heh."

The suggestions fly across the tabletop and waft upward with the heat and fumes emanating from the fading rocks. The moisture settles in around the Indian-written documentation of Indian competence spread out before the women warriors panting on their haunches around the

Formica table. They blink at one another, and the room smells of meat breath.

"Seeeey-maah!" calls out the keeper of the western door.

"More hot rocks!" they bark out in unison.

"Uh, the windchill factor out here is twenty-five below." The statement tentatively wafts in from the keepers of the outdoor fire, through the door flap of the sweatlodge, above the solid pitchfork that wields the massive, glowing boulder of volcanic history and women warrior tradition.

"Go to the gas station and get some hot coffee, for Chrissakes!" a voice growls from the southern door.

And the she-wolves hiss and yip as one.

"Seeeey-maah!" the keeper of the southern door calls out, or perhaps it is her guardian dodaim. No one is sure, because water and sacred plants are tossed on the glowing boulder, and the heat-holding moisture and acrid sulfur-laden smoke are contributing to oxygen deprivation, and the women warriors are yipping and singing and sharing secrets and ideas and strategies and coping mechanisms. They are reaching out and touching one another, nurturing one another, strengthening one another. They are making each other stronger. They are making each other bolder. They are licking one another's wounds, nibbling at one another's thick ears. They are wiping away the emotional and socioeconomic feces tossed their way by the Ugly One, empowered by Bean Boy, her friend and companion in ugliness and loneliness and the desperation of systemic, multigenerational, privilege-induced abuse.

The steam rises from this ritual cleansing, and the flimsy metal walls of the library-sweatlodge bulge and vacillate. Books and scholarly journals are exchanged, and coping mechanisms are crocheted like thick winter sweaters, heaped upon an accumulating pile of experience and determination and competence. There are books, letters, treaties, court cases, baby booties, and beaded moccasins. There are dictionaries and computers and fishing rights and baby blankets and textbooks and old sweetgrass baskets heaped upon the table of power that the she-wolves pace about and guard with those cold, yellow wild-dog eyes.

And the women warriors, armed and groomed for survival, once again lope out to their cars, their trucks, their tribal jobs a short walk down the road, their families, their obligations, and the expectations of a hate-filled community that has been filled with contempt for Indian people, once again, by a series of headlines about the poor performance and high truancy of incompetent Indians in an all-white educational system. They know better than to believe the lies and misconceptions and partial truths that are thrown their way by Shit Girl, the Ugly One. They know better than to present the truth and the studies and the statistics that have not been manipulated for a receptive audience of white-flight usurpers and haters. They know that such things will never be printed in Bean Boy's nonjournalistic trust-fund "newspaper" toy.

The scattering warriors toss generous bits more of wild tobacco to the winds and sing prayers for the offenders, no matter how far beyond hope of redemption and social adulthood they appear to be, and those women get on with the business of their lives. They cook and clean and bring home paychecks. They wash the dirt and the offensive nuances from their children's hair, and they braid into those long tresses magical things, like elk and windstorms and wild mustangs and '57 Chevys. And they teach their children how to care for these things, to groom them, and to keep them perfect for the next generation; because these things are more enduring and powerful than racism and self-loathing.

FROG WARRIORS

Omakakikwe arranged her schedule around the inconveniences that racism caused her on a daily basis. There was one post office that she did not go to. The clerk there called her a stinking Indian whore. Omakakikwe had married the farmer across the road from the farm his father had left to him and his brothers. She'd dared to act like a farmer, like she was equal to him and his brothers, even though she was a mere woman, an Indian woman with no inheritance of her own. That clerk knew, he knew better. His father had been an officer in the coast guard, and later in the air force. His older brother had been a staff sergeant in the army. He knew how things were ordered and ranked. He knew where that woman was supposed to rank. His brother once dated a girl who made friends with that Indian woman. She had no business being friendly with his brother's girlfriend when she crossed over the road to talk to her. She had no business crossing over that fucking road in turn and making friends with his brother's girlfriend. She should have known better than to cross over the fucking road. *Of course we can go over there — we're men who've inherited land and wealth. Our great-grandparents homesteaded this fucking county, because the stupid Indians lost some stupid war. There was more of it than those stupid Indians could use.*

And when my brother broke up with his girlfriend, that Indian whore had no business staying friends with her. And she had no business letting my brother's ex-girlfriend and her kids come to her house right across the road from our property, giving that bitch an excuse to drive down our road. So that Indian whore, that woman across the road who thinks she's as good as someone who's inherited something, she's got to be put in her place for letting my brother's ex-girlfriend think she's welcome in this neighborhood. Because being wel-

comed by a stupid Indian is not the same as being welcomed. My brother's ex-girlfriend, even though she's white, she's a whore, she's a gold digger, she's not welcome on our road.

Omakakikwe didn't go to that post office any more. She'd found that it cost a little more to mail her packages from that post office. She worried that maybe her mail might not get sent out from that post office. She worried that she might incite that postal clerk to further harassment, were she to merely show up and buy a stamp at that post office. So Omakakikwe drove a few miles out of her way to another post office.

Omakakikwe didn't go to the dentist in town any more. She went to one in another town. She'd missed an appointment for her son once, because she had seven part-time jobs, and keeping things like that straight was hard sometimes, when she was trying to keep straight at which job she was supposed to be and which mail she was supposed to respond to first. And the lady who worked in the front of the dentist's office talked to her like she was a dog. She made her feel like she wasn't welcome there any more. She made her feel like she was lucky they took her child as a patient at all, even though she had known the dentist all of her life. And this made Omakakikwe not want to take her child in for preventive care and maintenance. So she found a dentist in another town, farther from the reservation and farther from the assumption that Indians were dirt.

She and the boy always made a day of it, often rising at three or four in the morning to arrive for early morning appointments, to compensate for snow on the roads at certain times of the year. Even when the weather was nice, it would take two and a half hours to reach the dentist's office. Omakakikwe knew the back roads that skirted the rivers and lakes and avoided some of the busier towns and dangerous highway intersections. They developed a routine, the woman and boy, either packing a picnic lunch or stopping for a quick meal in one of the small towns. After each visit to the dentist, they would put gas in the truck, buy a small toy for the trip, or run other errands in the small town.

Omakakikwe had grown up outside this town, small and invisible as one of only a few Indians in its small Catholic school. Her father had provided for his family by helping to work the land that belonged to the large family of homesteaders he had married into. He also broke horses, caught from the once-logged, recovering pine barrens that harbored Michigan's last open grazing on state-owned lands. He was a tall man with hands so heavily calloused that he could roll hot coals around in his palms. He had bought a large parcel of land from his in-laws, a spectacular piece of several hundred acres, with a small, shallow lake completely within its borders. He had built barns, which he filled with rabbits, poultry, cows, small tractors, and other means by which the family put in extra hours to survive. Her mother made baskets out of black ash splints, from trees her father thinned for her next to the small lake. He would pound the logs until the growth rings popped up. Then Omakakikwe's mother would cut the thin wood into strips and smooth them with her old pocketknife. Sometimes she dyed the wooden splints with wild cherries or alder. Sometimes she would splurge and buy packaged dye from the five-and-dime store in town on Main Street.

Omakakikwe would take the boy to that same dime store, a safe and quiet place, still approachable once one navigated through the massive mini-malls and chain stores that met the needs of the growing population of whites escaping northward from the crowded urban centers of southern Michigan, where people of color huddled in unemployed and desperate masses, pressing out against the suburban ghettos of white uniformity and superiority. One time when Omakakikwe navigated the miles-long sprawl and coasted into the still-intact downtown, she lost herself in the nostalgia of her own small-town upbringing, where even an Indian child found a niche for brief periods of time. And, in a euphoric state of recalling the comfort of childhood, she bought her boy the biggest box of crayons she had ever seen. And for months the boy would lay them out on the crazy quilt his mother was perennially stitching that covered his bed. He would organize them by color, by hue, transitioning them according to the rainbow, or from lightest to darkest. He smelled them in big bundles in his small hands, before putting them carefully back into their holders and then into the big box that contained all of them. Omakakikwe would join him sometimes, and they would remember their adventures on those days that they traveled to and from the dentist to those hills in the highlands that composed the central backbone of the state, those days that they stepped outside of the racism that confronted them every day in their home community near the reservation along the shores of Lake Michigan, where miles of shoreline and a milder climate drew an even greater density of white people who sought to displace the simple Indians who would not mind moving and readjusting just one more time.

Along this long trek to and from the dentist, there was a favorite shallow pond on state land near the county road. One spring, they sat in the sunshine along its silty banks and watched toads sing for mates. The toads swam from log to log, from lily pad to lily pad, then blew their throats round and full, singing so long and loud that it made the two humans' ears hurt. Once, when they came to hear the toads, they encountered only small green frogs, the breeding season long over. Sometimes, later in the season, they stayed on the hillsides above that pond, filling their lunch cooler, their coffee cups, anything they could find, with red, ripe, ripe raspberries. And then they would hurry home to clean them before dark, saving some for a morning pie, freezing the rest for wintertime treats.

They went off on side roads, where Omakakikwe helped the boy duck under fences that had not been there during her childhood, and she would show the boy hillsides and deep lakes that now belonged to private lake associations. These were the marginal and sometimes-abandoned farm-lands of her childhood. She took the child once to the farm where her father had tried to build a life out of overlogged sand hills. She showed him a place to step over the barbed wire, where it had collapsed between the tidy trees of the soil-saving pine plantation she had helped her parents plant. She remembered whining a lot and not being very much help. She took him down the two-track that encircled the isolated lake, past the ruins of her own family home, which she did not point out to the boy. She stopped short of where she noticed a new house through the trees. And she remembered her father's untimely death and the lack of life insurance that transitioned a girl and her mother from hard-working survival to a total loss of home and assets. She remembered the white homesteader relatives who did not offer help, but who took the land back for nonpayment and sent the half-Indian woman and her girl back to the Indian community they had ventured from. She remembered her mother crying, after being called a freeloader. As an adult, Omakakikwe understood the use of the epithet as a premise for robbing her mother of the labor she had put in on the farm. The woman and child had been sent away without any compensation whatsoever from their white relatives, returning to the Indian side of their family empty handed. But loved. And Omakakikwe did not tell her own small boy about these things or about the stories of her family's presence in this place before even the homesteaders came. She merely described the hard work her tall, dark father had done. She did this from the cover of the forest, cowering down, knowing she no longer belonged there. She pointed out the sandbar where she used to swim. She told him how to catch and prepare turtles for cooking. She smiled when he said, "Eeeew. . . ."

She drove her son back to the pavement on back roads that had once belonged to her father. She showed him thin woodlots that had once been full of broad birch and maples and pines that her father had been grooming for future selective-logging operations. She showed him clearings around new natural gas–pumping stations, explaining the circumference and the special understory of the patches of virgin timber forest that had once lingered in those places. She pointed out small "potholes," ponds between lakes that had been considered insignificant, except by the turtle-and-frog-hunting Indians, the maple-sap-gathering Indians, the birch-bark-harvesting Indians. Now they were the private domains of grown-up trust-fund babies who resided in huge windowed wooden homes. She thought about her own small wood-heated home, the barns and workshops, the need to utilize and protect this whole place for miles in every direction. She tried to explain to the boy how many miles of land the elk needed, the bears needed, the grouse needed, even the frogs needed. Omakakikwe did these things on these trips to the dentist, taking advantage of the fact that she was intimidated by the white receptionists who protected their white dentists from clientele of color such as herself. . . . Omakakikwe knew how to make something special out of absolutely nothing.

Once, when the weather was beautiful and the sandy two-track roads that wound through the state forests were dry and driveable, she turned the truck onto a dirt road headed west. She remembered only vaguely the fairly straight gridwork of trails that went back and forth every couple of miles along the cardinal directions through this large plateau of gentle hills and interconnected potholes and small lakes. This tableland gave birth to the major rivers that drained the northern part of Michigan's lower peninsula, eventually becoming major waterways that emptied into Lakes Huron and Michigan. These days, they also gave birth to side roads that held private homesites for the lucky few who worked for the oil and gas companies that had been given access to Michigan's vast state lands in the decades since Omakakikwe had visited here with her parents.

The dense forests of tall pines and hardwoods were mostly gone, replaced by second-growth scrub and short, brushy, young plantation pines. The state's forests had been shaved completely from the face of the earth, sold off to make way for the oil and gas rigs—once it was realized that Michigan held such great reserves of underground wealth. Pipelines were housed in wide, straight swaths maintained through the brush, sprayed with defoliants to keep the persistent sumac, poplars, and birch from reclaiming the landscape. A few toxic berries persisted in the overly dry sunny spaces created by the herbicides. Countless pumping stations stood in great round clearings floored with gravel and concrete. Omakakikwe would periodically stop her truck in front of a great green pump, and she and the boy would stare in amazement through the chain-link fences at the silent, smooth motions of the tall machines.

Eventually, as they traveled away from the paved road, the woman and boy found themselves in woods that were somewhat more natural, though young and regrown, devoid of larger mature trees and moisture-preserving shade. These were "former" clear-cuts, although it seemed to Omakakikwe, who had known these woods in their former state, that they would never stop being anything but clear-cuts. There were no old, hollow trees to house woodpeckers and porcupines. There were no places left for bears to den. The few remnant elk had died off. The woodland buffalo had long vanished. The deer thrived and took over in unnatural proportions. In an attempt to appease newcomers who wanted access to public lands for recreational purposes but did not know how rich these lands had once been, the state had put in brightly posted all-terrain-vehicle trails. They crisscrossed the road in front of Omakakikwe's pickup truck, gutting the brush in every direction.

At one point she noticed the tops of young birch trees protruding along a ridgeline and anticipated that there would be a hollow with a small lake off in that direction. So she found a place to park her truck and suggested to the boy that they bring their lunch and sit by the water. The two of them had visions of singing back and forth with frogs and toads, staring down wary turtles, and throwing crumbs to eager minnows.

But what they found was not a lake. It was an empty hollow, wet and brushy in the middle, crisscrossed by deep tire tracks from recreational vehicles. She could see by the steepness of its sides and the alignment of the vegetation that this had once been a lake of several acres, deep enough for small fish and other water animals to survive long winters without freezing or loss of oxygen. It would have been just big enough to harbor both predators and prey, perhaps perch and aggressive bass or patient pike. Today it held a moist area no more than ten feet across, where a few wild irises struggled to survive. Even frogs could utilize this former lake in only the most transient manner. Perhaps high-pitched singing tree frogs might gather here for a few weeks at a time, after first ice-out. But larger toads, salamanders, turtles, fish, and fish-eating birds would find no reason to remain here through the dry summer.

Omakakikwe and the boy climbed up the opposite bank from that of their approach. There they found the trough of a well-used recreational vehicle trail, cut into the fragile soil a good four feet deep. They walked the tunnel, until it came back to the two-track they had had driven in on, and they returned to their truck in disappointment. There, they silently ate their peanut butter sandwiches, watching chickadees in the brush, through the windshield that now separated them from the reality of their loss.

Eventually, the two-track turned into a larger graveled road that wound downhill into a landscape of lakes and cottages and large new-looking homes with trees and moisture in the soil. There were pony barns that testified to the use the affluent made of the two-tracks and pipelines and the maze of pumping-station access roads. Soon things became more crowded, and signs for small businesses that serviced the summer people

and new permanent vacationers cropped up, along with a small convenience store near a fairly large lake.

In the midst of this, Omakakikwe saw a sign for a nonprofit nature
institute whose name she recognized. She had once accompanied a niece
on a class field trip to this facility, where the students had watched college
students from Michigan State University reenact seventeenth-century
Michigan life in an unlikely spot on the headwaters of the Manistee River,
where it was only about twelve feet across and a few feet deep. A young
woman portraying an Indian wore a fringed shirt of frayed bed-sheet
cloth, decorated with zigzags of various colors made with magic markers.
Her blond hair was held tight against her forehead by a beaded headband
that looked like the kind made in China. She politely explained that she
was not a real Indian (for which Omakakikwe was very grateful), and that
she was merely pretending to be an Indian for the purposes of the dem-
onstration. Then she held up a pair of commercially made snowshoes and
told how the Indians used them to travel.

Then the group shuffled down the path to the next station, where a
young woman dressed in traditional homesteader garb was tearing up
pieces of cotton cloth and striking a piece of flint and steel to show how
fires were made by the traders. She explained how superior this technology was to the way Indians started fires (which she didn't explain), and
then she explained how the Indians weren't as good at starting fires as the
white people, because they kept using pine needles and birch bark to light
fires with and hadn't figured out how much better cotton cloth was at getting fires started with a spark. And she stood there shredding up perfectly
good cloth, explaining how the Indians were amazed at the wives of the
fur traders and the homesteaders when they showed them this incredible
burning cloth.

So, instead of shuffling with the group up to the next reenactment station, where college students were dipping candles, Omakakikwe took the girl back down the trail to a place where birch and poplar trees grew in the sunshine by the river. And she popped a dark burned-looking piece of dry fungus from its host tree with a blow of her fist. "*Skwadaaginh,*" she said to the child. "*Skwadaaginh,*" the child repeated. Then they walked back to the girl in the long calico dress who was still fighting with the fabric, and Omakakikwe borrowed her flint and steel. With one long scrape, a spark fell onto the fungus. Omakakikwe blew, and the fungus glowed but did not flame. She explained to the young woman that a piece that size would probably glow for a good five or six hours, and that one didn't necessarily need steel to make a spark, and she thanked her for her nice presentation, before she and her niece shuffled back to the school bus.

Years later, Omakakikwe would buy a used computer from an electronics store, one that had been pieced together from various other used computers, and she would see the words "Manistee River Institute" pop up briefly every time she turned on the machine. She'd always thought she might contact the institute some time and see if they were interested in hiring an Indian to do a presentation. Because she knew that they were missing an awful lot. And she thought that maybe, as an educational institution, they might be interested in knowledge and history and a different perspective from the one they were accustomed to.

This day Omakakikwe and the boy were greeted initially by some enthusiastic young science interns who seemed pleased that they had been stumbled upon. Then Omakakikwe was referred to an older woman who was straight faced, rigid, without prosody in her speech. She explained how the institute existed singly to teach people about the beauty of nature as created by God. And the institution did not have time or money or mandate to take into consideration the traditions and history of one who had grown up with and learned about generations and centuries of survival in these woods. The primarily church-based private funding did not overflow into acknowledgement of Indian concerns. The woman pointed to the pond of accumulated water that persisted at the intersection of their uphill driveway with the built-up bed of the graveled county road and explained the ways they used it to teach classes about nature as God had intended it to be. And Omakakikwe could see that the classes were about nature as these people needed it to be. The woman explained how lucky they were to be located in the heart of this public land of stately forests. And Omakakikwe understood that this institute was about justifying the abuse of former forests for the oil and gas companies. The woman explained how generous the oil and gas companies had been in funding the institute. And Omakakikwe understood that this "educational" institution existed solely for the purpose of teaching people that this miserable remnant of habitat was what real wild nature was supposed to look like. It was about lowering the expectations of those new residents whose previous experiences had been primarily urban.

Omakakikwe and her boy found their way back to the highway, winding between the summer homes and the subdivisions and the increasingly thick human presence that choked out the frogs and the toads and the things that depended on small lakes and sloughs and potholes for food. And they sang frog songs for miles and miles. They stopped at the grocery store in that town close to the reservation, where they dared not feel comfortable going to a dentist or a doctor or a veterinarian. Then they headed up the hill to their own private sanctuary, their own small home. They sang frog songs for miles and miles. And, after the groceries were put away, they opened the windows, yearning for cool night air, to be greeted by unseasonable and resonant refrains of frogs and toads and toad-eating water birds. The calls grew persistent and dense, merging into one high-pitched tone. It was against this deafening song that Omakakikwe's family drifted off to sleep, wondering what the frog people expected of them, now that they had been privy to destruction that threatened more than mere Indians. They fell asleep with the joy of the song and the weight of responsibility for the messages that the song singers cried out from beyond their own window sills.

OK, so these three Indian women warriors walk into a bar. . . . Of course they don't! Because if they walked into that bar, when they walked out, they'd be stumbling drunk, and they'd step right into a Barbara Kingsolver novel, where they'd unanimously raise their infant children above their heads and give them away to a bunch of complete strangers, nice white ladies who just happened to be out for a stroll in the bar district of some major southwestern city or on their way to volunteer at the local Salvation Army; and the nice white ladies would have always admired the Native American culture, especially the nice parts of it where lovely long-haired children spend docile summers weaving birds' nests from wild branches in backyard thickets, and the ladies would have always secretly suspected that they were part Indian, because they understood Indian culture so much better than the angry, unemployed Indian parents they'd seen and read about, and in the end, the nice white ladies would all find out that they all had a secret Indian grandmother that they'd never met, and they were real Indians after all, and they therefore deserved to be able to properly raise beautiful, spotless, forever-well-behaved Indian babies who should fall into the arms of white ladies like them, especially since those Indian women warriors are always walking into bars.

Do you get it? Do you get it yet? It's a LIBRARY. The Indian women warriors are walking into a LIBRARY. And they've all been to college. And they can all read and write. And they are not alcoholics. They are loving, nurturing parents. And they have to work twice as hard at it as anybody else—because they've got a bunch of stereotypical images about them popping into people's minds, and they've constantly got to struggle against them.

OK, these women warriors, they stagger into the tribal library. It's been a rough week. Well, actually, it's been a rough month. Aw, hell, it's hard all the time. But that is the way life works, so these women warriors, they wipe their brows and they compose themselves, and they grasp the door handles to that library like they were grasping gilded railings on the wheelchair ramp up to Heaven.

And they keep coming, straggling in for a half an hour, putting their jobs and their errands and their parenting behind them. And they unload the coolers and the cardboard boxes full of food from the rusting cars that are paid for and the shiny cars that are not paid for. They plug a film about chimpanzees into the VCR, and they replace the liner in the wastebasket and set the clean one in front of their kids, and they place food and beverages and napkins into the hands of the children whose eyes are glued to the screen, and they scold final warnings to the ones who need it, and they pour themselves cups of hot coffee, and they pull the barrettes out of their hair. And they shake it down to their shoulders, where the elk and wild horses and '57 Chevys can get a foothold and take off at a gallop around the room, racing in a silent blur, first along the vinyl floorboards on the short, hard carpet, then up in the warm air above their heads, brushing cheeks and fenders against the cool glass of high windows that bring in the daylight and keep out the winter. And while the children safely watch a documentary about chimpanzees, those women warriors hum softly.

And they chuckle. And they exchange stories. And they glance at one another. And they catch reflections of themselves in the glass of a closed office door, where they see that they are beautiful. So they dance in a big circle around those children watching that documentary about chimpanzees, and they join their hands. First they dance to the right, for those who are happy. Then they dance to the left, for those who are sad. Then they dance back to the right again, because happy is better than sad. Then they dance to the left again, because they're really enjoying dancing like this.

But they don't always have as much control as they'd like over their lives, these women warriors, so they are a little bit superstitious, and they dance back to the right again, just to make sure they've tipped the scales toward happy. And then they fall on the short, hard gray carpet, giggling and still holding hands. But it might as well be long, soft grass on a summer day, because they can hear the wind in the trees and loving wavelets against the shore and a half a dozen different frog and toad songs roaring against the whisk of the traffic out there on the state highway that cuts through the center of the reservation and cuts them off from their few remaining feet of wetlands and beach. They can hear these things, these women warriors, and they are singing them to one another, teaching each other first the tunes, with gentle humming voices, then breaking into the syllabic comfort of tradition, then teaching one another the history and lives and natural history and interwoven nature of their own responsibilities as women warriors: keepers of the children, keepers of the sound of the waves on that beach, keepers of their own stories, keepers of the frogs and the elk and even wild horses and '57 Chevys.

And when they are done with this ritual, they bag up the paper plates and napkins and half-eaten cake scraps and vacuum the floor. They rinse the coffeepot, turn out the lights, and scatter for a few more weeks of exploration into the world of responsibilities that they will bring back and share at the next ceremony.

THE TRUTH ABOUT INDIANS

Shhhh. . . . Do you hear that? Do you hear that noise coming out of that building? They are like animals in there! Do you hear them? The ogitchi-daakweyag? Do you hear them? Those wimen warriors? They are primal. They are eeearthy.

You could be one, you know. No, I mean it, really. You could be one. I can tell. You seem special, you know, kind of spiritual. And if you buy my book, I'll let you in on all of their secrets. For a mere twenty-nine ninety-nine you could be one of them. Hell, I bet you could be better than them. I bet if *you* told Indian stories, they'd all have happy endings. I bet if *you* told the story about that dead bear over there, her tears would turn to honey gold and transform into islands out there in the lake. I bet if *you* told Indian stories, everybody's teardrops would turn into beautiful stones that children of all sizes and colors and denominations could pick up along the beach, especially the offspring of safe white parents who move up near the national park to get away from blacks and Mexicans and urban Indians down in the cities where those lovely children's parents built up lifetimes of wealth on the backs of those who earned less. That's right. I bet your Indian stories for non-Indians would be a whole lot better than theirs, those Indian women, the ones you hear howling over there in that little metal building. They sound like animals, don't they?

So you need to know what's going on in there, because you need some new ideas? Need some seeds for stories, some good *Indian* stories, public domain stories, don't belong to anybody? Read my book. C'mon, I'll show you the way. I'll tell you eeeverything. . . . Because I like you, you know, you seem nice. Kinda spiritual. I could tell the first time I met you. So here . . . for a mere twenty-nine ninety-nine, I can make you one of us. But don't tell anybody. It's a secret. I've printed up just this one volume, just for you. Didn't get it copyrighted or anything. Wouldn't matter if I did or not, because what's a copyright to an Indian, right? I mean, after all, we're *all* Native Americans, aren't we? I mean, anybody who's born here, we're *Native*, right? Because Indians, they're part of history, and it's *American* history, right? They've got a lot of nerve thinking they have a patent on that Native-to-America thing, don't you think?

Getting uppity, those Indian wimen warriors, aren't they? Starting to say things like *Anishinaabe* history, *Inuit* history, *Diné* history, *Lakota* History. . . . You can hear them in there, behind that sheet metal, inside that library there. *Tribal* library. Acting like they invented the idea of writing their own things down. Acting like they had education before the white man got here. Acting like they had books before the white man got here. Acting like they had stories before your grandparents homesteaded here. Acting like they had science and math and medicine before you moved up here from the cities. Acting like they wanted to fight their way out of poverty and deprivation of a place in modern history long before your home-site was selected from subdivisions of view lots, right up there above that bay there, just down the road from that nasty casino and those shitty tin-sided trailers they all work in. Acting like they have families and dreams and children and hopes. Acting human. Acting like they have as much right as you to be here. Getting greedy, aren't they?

You can hear them in there, howling. Like animals. Like welfare cheats. Like people who want something for nothing. Do you hear it? Do you hear it? I hear drumming in there. Do you hear that drumming? Think they've got a patent on that drumming, don't they? Those thin metal walls are shaking. They're probably in there complaining, strategizing. Maybe they'll think that they have the right to stay here and lower the quality of your schools. Maybe they'll think that they have the right to be here and lower your property values, make friends with those migrant farmworkers from that farm on the hill over there (you know, that nice farm that provides the scenery and open space views for the subdivision you live in), because those Mexicans, they're brown, too; make your neighborhood less safe. Helluva price to pay for a cheap head of lettuce, a cheap piece of fruit.

Maybe those Indians want to keep all that casino money to themselves, those Indians . . . use it for food program money. We know that it's mostly Indians who benefit from that food program money. Maybe use that casino money for tutoring. We know mostly Indians benefit from that tutoring. That money might better be used to buy fire trucks to protect your house way up on the hill over there in that view lot; after all, it's worth more than those little HUD houses and trailers and shit shacks those Indians live in. That's why they call it Shawby-town, that Indian village; sounds just like Shabby-town. Shabby people. Fish too much. Hunt too much. Almost as many deer are killed by Indians in this state as are killed by automobiles. It's a shame, isn't it? Because those deer, they're living out in those swamps and woods just so that they can walk right by your window up there on that hill over there, in that view lot. Pose for you, those cute deer.

And if you wrote the Indian stories, they'd be about nice girls who don't eat meat and would never, ever kill a poor defenseless deer, let alone cut one up for shoes or a purse or a buckskin-fringed dress when she plays the Indian at the annual lighthouse celebration put on by the historical society just up the state highway there. Because, for some reason, those Indians will not play Indian for you at your historical celebrations, where you celebrate yourselves and your brief presence in this place. They insist on doing it in there, behind those bulging, thumping tin walls, where you can't get a good look at everything. You can hear them in there, howling. Like animals. Like welfare cheats. Like people who want something for nothing. And, if you could get a good look at it, maybe you could even write a book about it.

So if you want those stories of yours to be authentic, you'd better buy my book, and I'll tell you what they're doing over there in the sweat-lodge — I mean the library — because I bet you can be an even better Indian woman warrior than any of *them* can any old day. Listen. Do you hear them howling over there? I can teach you to do that, and I bet you'd do it better than them. Because I can tell, you're special, kinda spiritual. Spirituality, clarity of thought, history, ties to this place — you too can have these things. Trust me. I promise. You can be a *real* Indian for only twenty-nine ninety-nine. (Plus tax.)

BABY STEALERS (BY PRESUMPTION)

They came in Volvo station wagons, along two-lane, freshly
     paved state highways. They came in Honda Civics that
         got forty-nine-miles-to-the-gallon. They came in
sleek black boats with seventy-horse-power-outboard-motors-
     that-leave-wakes-that-rock-the-pitiful-dinghies-of-
         the-Indian-fishermen. They came in cabin cruisers
with multiple engines that rocked the lakes that nurtured
     even the diesel fishing tugs of the most fortunate of
         Indian fishermen. They came in the-latest-
fashion-clothing and respect-commanding-brown-polyester-
     power-suits that impress only people like themselves.
         They came in shoo-in-jobs-with-less-than-
impressive-resumes from state colleges and universities
     that held them in high regard as warm bodies holding
         places for future generations of privileged white
middle-class suburbanites. They came with trust funds from
     affluent parents who had inherited opportunity and
         wealth.

They traversed long white beaches and abandoned farmsteads
     and insufficient highways that they dotted with
         subdivisions and multi-bathed-split-level-
dwellings-of-vinyl-siding-with-small-pony-barns-and-bird-
     feeders-next-to-the-cat-door-on-the-attached-garage.
         They came with custom-built log mansions that

mimicked rural inconvenience. They did these things because
they knew better how to use this land than the
Indians, who had, by virtue of their lesser
abilities, survived in mere tar-paper-shacks-of-
deprivation-and-hopelessness. Throwing trash out the
back door like they didn't have a car to take it
to the dump. Burning perfectly good trees to warm those
uninsulated hovels. Wasting perfectly good view lots.
Wasting perfectly good public parkland that
begged to be walked through, enjoyed, embraced by a more
appreciative audience, one with leisure.

They came through miles and miles of tidy-farms-whose-
migrant-farmworker-shacks-sat-out-of-sight-and-empty-
for-much-of-the-year. They came to gleaming,
white public schools, from which Indian children were
safely sent away to the last Indian boarding school in
the United States, up there, safely far away on
that island, safely distant from the mainland mainstream
children they might contaminate by their presence.
Shhhh . . . didn't call it an Indian Boarding School,
called it a Reform School, but we knew who went there.

They came expecting it all to stay white and perfect for
them to enjoy in perpetuity. They never dreamed that
those Indians might fight to bring their children
home, might fight for the right to earn a living, might
fight for the right to harvest those resources that
were theirs by treaty, might fight for the right

to walk the streets without fear or to-be-seen-in-public.
They did not anticipate lawyers and statisticians and
researchers and educators. They did not
anticipate loving parents and guardians of traditions. They
did not anticipate warriors.

WIMEN WARRIORS ARE NOT BORN, THEY ARE TRAINED

Niwezo'on is nervous. She is nervous because her oldest child is attending the local junior college. She is grateful that the child is saving money by taking classes close to home in preparation for going away to university, where things cost a lot more, and children are more vulnerable to economic and emotional predation. And she is grateful that the child comes home each night to the safety of her arms and the safety of her support and warriorlike mentality. But she is fearful for the time the child is on the roads, a myopic and inexperienced rural driver in a congested place full of other inexperienced drivers converging on the same zigzagged parking lot. But mostly she is afraid for the child's psyche. Attending a public educational institution is a risk factor for suicide for young Native Americans. The death rate goes up with each year in attendance. Niwezo'on has had to put every bit of spare energy available into preparing the child for the psychological onslaught of abuse that will be heaped upon her. She has had to train the child in the martial arts of self-respect and dignity. She has taught the child the smooth, flawless moves of walking away, saying nothing, letting the foolish think of themselves as superior. She has taught the child how to preen feathers, spread wings, and rise above the institutional racism. She has armed the child. She has armed the child with oral history. She has armed the child with tradition. She has armed the child with self-worth. But still, Niwezo'on is nervous.

She putters. She goes to her seasonal job cleaning toilets at a nearby lodge. She cannot afford to pass up the opportunity for a few dollars, so she can pay the salaries of those important college instructors whose credentials do not exceed her own. She stays on call to help lift road kill off the highway for the county, so that she can pay for the medical and dental benefits of those important college instructors whose credentials do not exceed her own. She takes seasonal work shipping Christmas packages from a sweatshop, so that she can provide paid sick-leave and vacations for those important college instructors whose credentials do not exceed her own. And she teaches her own child to emulate those college instructors, so that she will not be perceived as just another Indian, one who might be expected to clean toilets for those important college instructors whose credentials do not exceed her own.

And the child calls from only twenty-five or so miles away, and she asks, Mom, have you heard of this book?

No.

Mom, have you heard of this author?

No. No, this is not someone that Indian people read. Indian people have been reading for education. Indian people have been reading for self-defense. Indian people have been reading to try to become something other than cleaners of toilets for those college instructors whose credentials do not exceed their own. But Indian people have not been reading for entertainment.

And the child explains that the people in her sociology class have been asked to read this novel, about Indians, so that they can understand some of what Indians go through. But the book, Mom, it doesn't seem right. It makes me feel bad about myself. There is something wrong with this book, Mom. We're supposed to write about this book, Mom, and I don't know what to write. I'm bringing the book home for you to look at. And the child leaves the pay phone, leaves her connection to reality that the book had made her yearn to reach out and reaffirm.

Niwezo'on flips through the book. She reads in the middle, and it doesn't make any sense. She reads in the beginning, and it doesn't make any sense. She reads all the way to the end, and it doesn't make any sense.

"Why would an Indian get drunk and give her baby away?" the daughter asks.

"It's beyond me," answers the mother.

"It doesn't say anything about it in the book."

No. No, it doesn't. It says nothing in that book about hatred, hoarding of resources. It says nothing in that book about displacement. It says nothing in that book about underemployment. It says nothing about the sharp knife blade of discrimination in hiring that rests against the throats of Niwezo'on and her family. It says nothing about how hard Niwezo'on worked to teach her child how to survive among those college instructors whose credentials do not exceed her own. It says nothing about how the child had assured her, "Don't worry, Mom, I'll learn to be like them. I'll get a job among them. I'm not as dark as you. [I'm not as Indian in mentality as you.] I can pass." The book says nothing about the imposition of socioeconomic difference that made Niwezo'on give away that little piece of her child, drunk or not.

The book talks about the white ladies into whose deserving arms a lovely Indian child fell and what a swell job they did of making her into a better Indian than the kind that gives away perfectly good light brown babies. (If they spent enough time out in the sun, they could probably even pass her off as their own.) The book talks about how those ladies turned out to be part Cherokee or Choctaw, or one of those southeastern tribes driven westward that America knew by name and fell to out of convenience when they needed to invent a romantic ancestor. And those ladies gave their Indian child a really cool Indian name—Turtle—like she was slow, maybe, and needed white mentorship; like she was spiritual, nonhuman, part animal, *exotic*. Like that child could make her white mentors special by mere association.

OK, this Indian woman warrior walks into a library. A *library*, got that? Not a bar. A library. It's the tribal library. And she stomps over to the desk, where there's this box of books on the floor that has been donated to the library by a well-meaning white person who probably works for the tribe. The box has been sitting there for two months. Niwezo'on had shuffled through the box of books sitting there waiting for the white part-time head librarian to come in and add them to the collection. And there it was, the second book down, a single-bound collection of that trilogy by Barbara Kingsolver, the one that contains the story about the Indian woman who came out of a bar drunk and gave away her baby to somebody who the author apparently thought would appear to be a better parent for an Indian child, even though her credentials probably did not exceed those of the mother. And Niwezo'on had muttered to the full-time Indian librarian's assistant that this was a bad book that hurt Indians and that it needed to be burned or put in a back corner of the room with a warning label on it, kept perhaps only as an example for someone doing research about damaging stereotypes about Indians in contemporary literature.

But the Indian librarian's assistant looked wide eyed at her fellow warrior; she looked sideways at the white tribal teacher who was busy across the room. She looked at the books. She whispered, "We're guests here. We can't afford to make waves." (It was, after all, a printed document, a piece of formal Americana that a mere Indian dare not interfere with or question the validity of, let alone destroy.)

Niwezo'on has been thinking about the words that child said to the mother when she took the initiative to tell her college instructor why a book about an Indian woman getting drunk and giving away her baby promulgated disparaging ethnic stereotypes. Niwezo'on has been thinking about how the child thanked the mother for giving her strength and self-esteem for the days she drove in to the junior college and did battle against the status quo of institutional ignorance. And she realizes that the child chose to stay whole, that the child would not let the mother give away even one small piece of her. (It also helped that the child found a negative review of the novel by Sherman Alexie on the Internet that she could send in along with her paper, just so that college instructor didn't have to give too much weight to the opinion of just one young woman warrior whose credentials probably would not ever surpass his own.)

And now, three weeks later, this Indian woman warrior walks into a library. And she plucks that book up from where it has been sitting in that untouched box. She wipes the dust off its cover. She shuffles through the top drawer of the librarian's desk for a permanent marker. She selects one, wide and dark and fresh. And she writes, deliberately, carefully, boldly across the cover: THIS BOOK IS BAD FOR INDIANS. IT PROMOTES DAMAGING STEREOTYPES THAT HURT US IN SOCIOECONOMIC TERMS. WE HAVE NOT BEEN GETTING DRUNK AND GIVING OUR BABIES AWAY TO MORE-DESERVING WHITE LADIES — AND WE'RE NOT GOING TO START NOW.

And she writes it again just inside the front cover. And inside the back cover. And she flits through the pages and writes it six more times over the text in various places, evenly spaced and hitting all three volumes of the trilogy, so that no one can miss it. And then she lightly touches the white male tribal schoolteacher on the shoulder and politely says, "If you ever want to have one of your students do a term paper on damaging stereotypes about Indians and how they contribute to racism in hiring and education and other cultural venues, this book would be a really good place to start. I'm going to put it on that shelf over there." And she throws it in the wastebasket.

And, you know what? It's OK. That white guy that teaches for the tribe, he's a really nice guy. And those wimen warriors, they're starting to rub off on him a little bit. And he doesn't even seem to mind. It's like that wit' dem wimen warriors, dey sneak up on ya. Really, they do.

BABY STEALERS (UNINTERRUPTED)

She'd been taught from birth to keep her head down. Even
her mother had been taught before her birth that she
had had no business conceiving her. She was,
after all, a child of color, born of a woman of color who
had no business breeding, who had no business
attaching herself to a white man who would no
more give her the time of day than a whore on a street
corner, or attaching herself to a man of color who
could no more give her the time of day than a
white man. She was born into a world that wanted nothing of
brown skin, nothing of brown hair, nothing of brown
eyes, nothing to remind the world that she
represented a culture that should have disappeared and had
no business hanging on, except as an adjunct to the
dominant culture and to serve.

Defeeeeated. Her people had been defeeeeated. Fair and
square. In a war. No matter that they did not elect to
participate in that war. No matter that they
chose peace and nurturing and education over war. They had
had resources. And by the very nature of being
possessors of resources, they'd opened themselves
up to usurpation of those resources. They'd had no business
even considering possessing resources, her people. And
they'd had no business even dreaming that their
offspring would be entitled to those resources.

That's the way it was with those resource usurpers. They
came in various forms. Came in different waves. Came
as explorers. Came as traders. Came as slave-
traders. Came as pilgrims. Came as immigrants. Came as
miners. Came as farmers. Came as refugees. Came as
philosophers. Came as professors. Came as
businessmen. Came as employees. Came as superior. Came to
take. Came to take. Came to take.

YA BETTER WATCH DEM WIMEN WARRIORS

See that woman over there? Yeah, see her. She belongs to da wimen's warrior society. Yeah, I know, she don't look like it. But don't be fooled. Dey
full-bloods. Dey half-breeds. I even met some of 'em only quarter-bloods.
It only depends on how the outside world sees them. Once an Indian, always an Indian.

And that one there, she does some pretty sneaky shit. Better watch
out for that one there. She's smart. You can't trust her, she's smart. She
don't take nothin' from nobody, that warrior, that one. Maybe listens to
da odder wimen warriors sometimes, but mostly she don't listen to nobody, dat one. She's like a fucking snowplow, that one. Like a moose goin'
through a deep drift with long legs, dat one. Like a pike slippin' through
the water weeds, that one. Like a catfish on da bottom of a river, dat one.
Like a raccoon on the far side of a tree. Like a coyote, like a wolf, like a fox
at dusk, that one. Like a bobcat in the snow. Like a heron in the top of a
birch tree. Like a falcon on a breeze. Like a trout at a rivermouth. Sneaky
as shit. Knows how to survive.

Think you can make her dependent on you? Think again. Think you
can make her need you? Think again. Think you can make her need your
technology? Think again. That one, she can live without a phone, can live
without electricity, can live without a paycheck, can live without your approval. That one, she's sneaky as shit. Knows how to survive.

Think she needs your schools? Think again. She can make a school
out of nothin'. She can make a school out of the wind. She can make a
school out of the sky. She can make a school out of fishing rights, out of a
Supreme Court decision, out of your throwaways, out of your dirty socks,

your spit, your laundry, your garbage, your expectations, your ambitions. She can turn those things back on you. She can. She sure as shit can. Because she's used to doing more with less. And when you get uncomfortable, that woman warrior, she'll just look at you and say, "Aaah, just right." When you think you got the fire hot enough you can push her out of the frying pan, she says, "Mmmm . . . nice and warm." When you think it's cold enough you can push her out the door and say, "Freeze, suffer, be cold and miserable," she just looks up and says, "Oh, yeah, I was gettin' too hot from workin' so hard." So you gotta watch them, them wimen warriors, 'cause they're sneaky as shit.

You say, "Go ahead, suffer, live without a dishwasher," and she look at you, say, "Hey, I never had a dishwasher." You say, "Go ahead, suffer, live without a telephone," and she look at you and say, "Hey, I never had a telephone when I was growing up, can live without one now." And you was thinkin' that maybe you was better than her, because you had a dishwasher and a telephone, and she's just goin' along just fine without them things. And maybe you're gonna suffer more than her without them.

See that one there? She knows how to make baskets. Knows how to peel a tree, make them baskets. Knows how to pluck quills off a dead porcupine, decorate them baskets. Not like you. You, you gotta wear them polyester suits. Can't get porcupine blood on them polyester suits. Can't get tree bark on them polyester suits. She can work until her arm is stiff and sore. Not like you. You can't work until that arm is stiff and sore. Can't slide in and out of them polyester suits if that arm is stiff and sore. She can swap them baskets for stuff. Swap them for food. Swap them for money. Swap them for music lessons for her kids. Makes them good at math, them music lessons. You can't swap that polyester suit for music lessons. Can't swap that polyester suit for math. Can't swap that polyester suit for anything but pretending to be better than an Indian. And that only works in *your* neighborhood. Don't work in the rest of the world. Don't work in the snow. Don't work in the cold. Don't work in the heat. Don't work in hard times. Don't replace hard work and ingenuity, that polyester suit. So you better be careful. Better watch out. Better keep your distance, 'cause dem wimen warriors, they can catch a fish, clean a fish, eat a fish, be a fish, and you be standin' there in polyester, not knowin' what hit ya.

THE WARRIOR IN THE MERCEDES

I knew this Indian guy once, really sweet. He used to tell these dumb jokes that the little kids liked, but the big kids always thought they were dumb. He was maybe ten years older than me, this guy. Coulda passed for white, this guy. But he didn't. Maybe his mum was Indian, so he couldn't. Couldn't escape the accusations that she'd married a white man for his money. Or couldn't escape the accusations that she'd bred with a white man for the advantages, in the hopes of making her offspring white. Didn't matter why it happened, because it was a no-win situation. But, this Indian guy, he was half white. And he would never, never in his life ever be known as this white guy. He would always, all of his life, be known as an Indian guy. Even though he was half white. And even though he could pass.

He'd grown up in the city, this Indian guy. It happens to a lot of them. There is nothing for their Indian parents back in the rural counties they came from. Fishing gone. Lumber gone. Jobs never an option. So maybe that Indian parent marries somebody else, marries a white person. Maybe does it out of love. Happens, y'know. People sometimes they marry out of love. Or maybe it happens because that one parent hopes to tap in to that privilege that comes with race, that automatic affluence and benefit-of-the-doubt that comes with lighter skin. They do that because they do not know about the brown-paper-bag rule — gotta be lighter than a brown paper bag, unless you live in L.A. or Florida. They do that because they do not know about the one-drop rule — once colored, always colored. Can't wash that colored parent's influence off you. It's like permanent dirt. Or maybe it just happens by accident, because we are sexual beings, and it is an awfully strong biological urge, that procreation thing, happens whether you plan it or not. Whatever the reasons (although I like love the best), that mixing, that blending—it happens. And the people who come out of it, they are people. They are real people. They have hopes. They have dreams.

And this Indian guy, he had hopes. He had dreams.

He'd gone to college, and he'd studied education. And he'd actually taught somewhere, in some big city where nobody else would teach, and where he'd passed for white for a while. And he'd gotten hopeful, and he'd gotten his doctorate in education. Half of all Indians get their doctorates in education. Odd thing, when you consider that it's not a very integrated profession, especially when you move up the pecking order into admin- istration. . . . But this Indian guy, he'd messed up and told somebody that he was an Indian, so he got shuffled into graduate programs in education, because that's where Indians get shuffled—on account of people think Indians are not educable, and they think that Indians should become ed- ucators of Indians, in the hopes that some mysterious new standard that allows integration will erupt on the surface of the field of education, like a boil that needs popping. But it is intended to be nothing more than a boil, because the surface appearance of education must never change.

So this guy, this half-Indian guy, he was pretty cute. He was short. And he never raised his voice. And he smiled all-the-goddam-time, because he could not afford to appear to be even slightly competent or firm or in charge, lest he overstep his boundaries as a token Indian in a system-that-would-not-consider-the-option-of-change. He grew his hair long, kept it that way, in a ponytail, so he could look like a cute Indian. And he drove a gray Mercedes, so he could look like a school administrator, a man of success, someone-who-made-more-than-the- average-guy-and-was-therefore-allowed-to-make-decisions-for-people- about-their-children. Only this Mercedes, it was kind of old. And the bottom was all rusted out, and this Indian guy, he never made enough money to get a little body work on that fancy car or get it painted, because white jobs like public school administrator, or even bottom-end-of-the-market-entry-level-teaching-with-a-bachelor's-degree, were not available to him. But he was smart. So he used silver duct tape all along the bottom of that silver Mercedes Benz to make it look good. And it looked good at a distance, which is all you need to impress somebody from a school board or an administrator's office, because they do not step outside and get their shoes gooey.

But the Indians saw it. They saw it up close, because whenever he visited the Indians, they walked him out to his car, and they helped him carry all the food and gifts and stuff that they gave to other Indians whenever they showed up on their doorsteps. The Indians saw that duct tape. And they giggled, because they knew what it was like to try to impress the people who could not be impressed, the ones who were too set-in-stone in their prejudice and their assumptions-that-they-were-better-than the Indians that they moved north and tolerated. And those Indians, they were sad for this guy, because they knew what it was like to try to impress the people who could not be impressed, the ones who were too set-in-stone in their prejudice and their assumptions-that-they-were-better-than the Indians they moved north and tolerated. And they were hurt, the Indians, because they knew that such exercises were mere futility, that time and effort and hopes and dreams would always be wasted on trying to impress the people who could not be impressed, the ones who were too set-in-stone in their prejudice and their assumptions-that-they-were-better-than the Indians they moved north and tolerated. And they were angry, the Indians, because they knew that their own time and effort had been wasted in the past, and that that learning would simply go to waste, because here was just one more Indian trying too hard and never succeeding.

And he came home from the city, that Indian guy. Found a bunch of other Indians. Got a job with the tribe, making pennies-on-the-dollar compared to a white guy with his credentials. And he married this beautiful Indian woman with a beautiful Indian child. And he was a soft and loving and powerless parent and husband. And he was a strong and masterful and ingenious parent and husband. And if you think for just one minute that all warriors are women, you'd better grab yourself by the cerebellum and you'd better rethink that notion. You'd better comb that notion out of your hair. You'd better shake it from your clothing, wash it from your bedding. You'd better wad up that silly notion and toss it out the door on a windy day. Take it out on a big lake in a small boat and set it adrift.

Because warriors come in many, many shapes and sizes. And all warriors deserve respect.

THESE WARRIORS, THEY WALK INTO A SWEATSHOP

OK, this woman warrior, she walks into this sweatshop for a job, because she can't get a job commensurate with her credentials. . . . It doesn't matter what kind of a sweatshop it is that she's looking for. It could be a temporary job as a bus aide taking care of the physically disabled kids of the migrant farm workers exposed to toxic doses of pesticides and herbicides, the ones who will head south to Texas in a few weeks after school starts. That particular job would end up paying less than the gas she would spend jumping through the hoops to get it. She'd actually lose money on that particular job. But the white people whose college diplomas are no more significant than hers, but who work at that school district making living wages with medical and dental benefits, they will never know the difference. In fact, they will not care, and they will assume that people of color and the less fortunate are determined to supplement their success by working for less than it actually costs them to show up to work. Those educators will assume that they are being supplemented by volunteers who accept their superiority.

Maybe this job this woman warrior walks into will be in a sweatshop that packs up holiday packages for parents who do not have the time to bake cookies for their children in college, the ones who are studying to be public school administrators or school teachers or college instructors or managers at car rental businesses who will act nervous about renting cars to Indians. But the people who buy those services will assume that whoever is packing up those goodies and snacks for far less than they themselves can live on are doing so out of choice, because they somehow elect to supplement and embellish the lives of those who are more deserving of embellishment than themselves.

Or maybe this job will be in a museum sweatshop, where affordable Indian trinkets must be made available at third world prices so that the museum gift shop remains profitable, and the staff of the museum can continue to take home tolerable wages with benefits and retirement. And this particular gift/sweatshop will teach more to the museum's visitors about stratification in society than the museum exhibits will teach about the histories of various cultures. And maybe this museum gift/sweatshop will hurt Indian people more than it will celebrate them. But it will never have been about benefiting the Indians.

Maybe this woman warrior will walk into a casino sweatshop, where she will be asked to deal the cards to a cigarette-smoking, flashing-lights-celebrating audience, shuffling and sliding each ace and deuce to the thrum, thrum, thrum of the rock music that drowns out thoughts and dreams and makes the time pass like fluid light, makes the childhoods of her Indian children pass like hazy wishes, makes her college training and her years of striving pass like ambitions that were never meant to be realized.

Maybe this woman warrior will seek work in a federal Indian education grant sweatshop, where she will be asked to work for small wages in an on-call capacity, with no set working hours or guaranteed income or workers' compensation insurance. And in this sweatshop she will wonder if she will make more than the cost of her gas and the double share of her self-employment taxes in exchange for her time and effort every time she leaves for "work." This particular sweatshop would leave scars on her image of self, convince her that she is valuable only to the extent that a federal grant is available, worthless when it fades away. It would send her the message that she exists only to supplement those from a loftier socio-economic strata who are more deserving of full-time employment with benefits and retirement and future security than she is, because of some innate quality that makes her lesser.

Maybe this woman warrior will walk into a lodge or a motel or a resort, where she will ask for the opportunity to clean toilets or wash dishes during the summer months when the lakes are swimmable and the rivers are fishable and the beaches and woods are walkable and the skies are touchable. And the summers of her own children will pass like wispy dreams and ambitions too big for words. And this sweatshop will tell the warrior that she dare not claim ownership to summertime and warm breezes and clean, clear streams and lakes. Or fantasies like college diplomas and economic success or career satisfaction or pride in one's own accomplishments.

OK, this woman warrior, she walks into the tribal library, and she says, "Shhhh. . . . Stop complaining. This is as good as it gets. We are the underpeople. This is how we are supposed to live."

And the other women warriors, they stop short. They lose track of their coffee cups. There is a crashing and a sloshing of warm fluid and nondairy creamer. Eyes flash and fluorescent lights flicker. Clouds fly dark and heavy from west to east. Cold winds bite and tear at the glass doors and thin siding of the building. The atmosphere within the room bulges and swells, and the women pivot. The barrettes are falling loose from their hair of their own accord. The elk tear free from brown and graying tresses and spring from the women's shoulders. Wild mustangs of every pattern and color leap down to paw at the short, hard gray carpet. They lower their heads and stare into the yellow headlights of '57 Chevys, and those horses, they flare their nostrils. They breathe heavy. And those Chevys, they race their engines, and they spew bobby socks and sparks and exhaust from their tailpipes. Small children squeal and run in every direction. Teenagers gasp and clutch their computer mouse pads, while windstorms circle the cluster of plugged-in desktops.

The keeper of the eastern door does not wait patiently for the next fire to be lit in the bowels of the sweatlodge of aluminum and vinyl and polychlorides and paper and stereotypes and broken promises. She looks around at the young faces in the room. She looks at the exasperated mothers. And she strolls, long armed and loose, from the table near the head librarian's office, the one that is covered with military recruitment brochures that she has been slowly slipping into her coat pocket one at a time, so that nobody will notice, taking them home and throwing them into the pile of papers she uses to light fires in her woodstove.

"Hey, you know, you guys, there's this song, this paddling song. I learned it from Anny up in the Sault. And she learned it from her granny. And me 'n Anny, we're both the same age, so this song, it ain't gettin' any fresher. So maybe I better teach it to you now. Gather round. Listen up. This is a clan song. This is the song from the Turtle People. They're fish clan, those Turtle People. And that's a really big clan, that fish clan. Got all kinds of critters in it. What kind of creatures do you think are in that fish clan, besides the obvious, besides the fish?"

"Crayfish."

"Yeah. Yeah, you're right. I know a really good crayfish story. Maybe I'll tell it to you later."

"Frogs."

"Yeah. Yeah, frogs. Important, those frogs. Feed a lot of birds and fishes, those frogs. Got some really important jobs to do, those frogs. I know a really good frog story. Funnier than the crayfish story, even. Maybe I'll tell it to you later."

"You gonna teach us the paddling song, or what?"

"Yeah. Yeah, I'm gonna teach it to you. I got some good paddling stories, too. I know one that's funnier than the crayfish story, funnier than the frog story. Good story, that canoe story. Maybe I'll tell it to you later."

"You ever sing this song paddlin' a canoe?"

"Yeah. Yeah, I've sung this song paddling a canoe. It makes you paddle pretty fast, because it's got a good steady beat. Some of you are study-

ing music. You should learn this song. This song is a mathematical mas-
terpiece. This song is about breaking up the spaces and times and empty
spaces between the strokes. It is about fractions."

"Do you want me to go get my drum?"

"Naw, naw, thanks for offering. But I think we ought to start out this
song real quiet. Think like we are on the lake."

"Which lake?"

"Your favorite lake. Shut up and paddle."

"He's not paddling."

"Just worry about yourself. Don't mind what's going on in the next
canoe. You keep messing around worrying about everybody else, twisting
this way and that, you're gonna slow down your own canoe. You're gonna
paddle into a stump, maybe hit a rock. . . . Sun's shinin'. Nice day. Shut up
and paddle, like your mother tells you to."

"Where are we goin'?"

"Doesn't matter. Just listen to this song. This song is like the 'Mary
Had a Little Lamb' of Anishinaabe culture. Everywhere you go, you gonna
be hearing this song, maybe one version of it or another, a little faster, a
little slower, maybe another couple of notes added. This is an important
song. You really oughta know this song. Chi chi, chi chi bwa-aanh. Chi chi
bwa-aanh."

"That's it?"

"What? Were you expecting a Beethoven sonata? It's a paddling song.
Shut up and paddle."

"Is there more to the song?"

"Yeah. Yeah, there's more to the song. Shut up and paddle."

"You know any Beethoven stories?"

"You ever been smacked with an imaginary canoe paddle?"

THE WARRIOR AND THE OBJECTIVE PRONOUN

"I want to hear the frog story."

"Not now. Maybe later."

"Why not?"

"We've gotta do objective pronouns."

"But we already did objective pronouns."

"But you don't remember objective pronouns. So we've got to do them again.

"What's the frog story about?"

"The frogs and the toads mess up, and they get busted."

"Who busts them?

"Manaboozhou. Manaboozhou busts *them*. That is the objective pronoun."

"Why?"

"Because it's not the subject. It's in the predicate part of the sentence, the part of the sentence that defines the action. It stands for the object or the indirect object of the sentence. Manaboozhou busted *them*."

"Why?"

"For stealing."

"What did they steal?"

"Mostly they stole nuts and berries. Nuts and berries, those are the direct objects in that sentence. They stole nuts and berries. Turn it into an objective pronoun."

"They stole *them*."

"Good."

"What were a bunch of frogs and toads gonna do with a bunch of nuts and berries?"

"What were they going to do with *them*."

"Yeah, yeah, what were they going to do with *them*?"

"Well, back then frogs and toads had teeth."

"Were they vampires?"

"No. If they were vampires, they would've gotten busted for stealing blood. They would have had to have taken *it* from other animals. They would have had to have taken *it* from *them*."

"Or . . . they could have been given *it*, by *them*."

"When did you start listening?"

"To *what*?"

"Hey, I think that might be interrogative, too."

"Maybe it could be both."

"Which one would we answer on a test?"

"I'd go with the obvious. I'd go with interrogative."

"But, isn't it both?"

"Yeah. But they're probably not going to give you the choice of picking two answers on the test. Unless it says so on the directions. You always gotta read the directions."

"So the frogs and toads had teeth."

"Lots of 'em. . . . They had lots of teeth. They had *them*."

"Why?"

"So they could chew their food! . . . So they could chew their food with *them*."

"Big deal."

"Yeah, well Manaboozhou, he was keeping an eye on them (on *them*). Because, at first, they were just stealing from each other. You could hear them over there in that little swamp by the stream behind the health center. They were bickering. They were name calling. Thief, thief! You stole my wild plums! And those bullfrogs, they went, *kung, kung, kung.* And those green frogs and those brown toads, they trilled an awful lot. And the tree frogs and the little leaf toads, they peeped their lungs out. Whoo boy, it was noisy!

"So Manaboozhou, he comes over to take a look, see what's causing all of this commotion. And he sees that this one big toad is bigger than all the other frogs and toads, and he's just being this horrible pig and he's stuffing his face."

"Can I go get some chips?"

"Jeeeezzz, no! That's how the whole thing started!"

"You said it was berries and nuts."

"Well, yeah, at first it was. But then they started stealing from other animals, too. Took seeds from the birds — especially those tree frogs. Took grains from the ground squirrels, grass seeds from the mice.

"And Manaboozhou, he climbs up this big swamp maple next to the water, and he looks down, and he sees it's really a mess down there.

"And he's eating this big bag of chips — "

"What kind of chips?"

"Doritos. And he sets this bag of chips down in the crotch of this tree, and he says, 'Hey, you guys, it's me, Manaboozhou, and I'm tellin' you to quit doin' that.'

"And these frogs and toads, they're really into it, all the name calling, and they're throwing everybody's nuts 'n berries back and forth at each other, yellin', 'Take your dumb old chokecherries. I didn't want them anyways.' And this one green frog, he spits out this wild cherry seed, and it hits this tree frog right in the eye.

"So right away, Manaboozhou, he's gotta fix this. So he puts these spots on the backs of those humps on the frogs' and toads' heads, and they look like they got eyes on the back, so now nobody can tell if they're coming or going and nobody can intentionally hit them in the eye. And he's really proud of himself for doing this, and he sits back and reaches for his bag of Doritos . . . and it's gooone."

"Darned tree frogs."

"You're tellin' *me*!"

"So what did Manaboozhou do?"

"He took all their teeth away. That's right, he took *them* away from *them*. Made them spit *them* out into a basket.

"Manaboozhou, he reached around like this, holding out that basket, and he said, 'OK, now, spit them out, you guys.' And they spit *them* out."

"Did any of them spit *them* out at *him*?"

"Yeah. Yeah, but that's another story."

"*Now* can I get some chips?"

"Yeah. Just don't let me catch you stealing any from one another."

"Aaw, ow! I just hit myself in the eye with a Dorito!"

"*Whom* did you just hit in the eye?"

"Interrogative."

"*Myself*. I just hit *myself* in the eye."

"Reflexive."

"Get your hands off those Doritos. They're *mine*."

"Possessive."

BABY STEALERS (BY INDIFFERENCE)

It wasn't supposed to be a quilt. It had never been
        conceived of as anything more than a repair job, a quick
            fix, a temporary solution to temporary poverty.
She had merely intended to mend an old flannel bed sheet,
        itself pieced out of older flannel bed sheets and
            inherited from her mother. But racism in hiring
had left her bereft of options when she woke up and tried
        to figure out how to be productive on any given day.
            So she started to mend the sheet.

She'd tried finding newer, less-worn sheets at the thrift
        shops in the nearest city. But the urban poor always
            beat her to those things. And she supposed it was
all right, because they were probably single mothers,
        struggling for survival themselves. Or perhaps they
            were handicapped people. Or refugees. There were
any number of people that America had taught her were more
        valuable than she was. Do not despair for yourself,
            America had told her, because there are those who
have even less than you. There are people who do not have
        electricity. And being a good student of world
            citizenship, she took this directive seriously.
She treated her limited access to electrical power with
        reverence and considered it a godsend, a gift, a
            privilege. And she paid her electric bill on time
whenever she could.

The flannel bed sheet had worn thin, so thin that the
family members put their feet through it at the weak
spots. Those places had become too threadbare to
merely stitch. So she added pieces from almost equally
threadbare flannel work shirts that had frayed and
torn and thinned in places, but yielded enough
solid fabric to mend the weak spots in that old flannel
sheet. So she began the game of catch-up, trying to
mend the lifeless parts of the old fabric with
almost-as-old fabric that itself had a short lifespan.
Eventually she was able to add stronger pieces of
fabric—patches from old blue jeans, themselves
patched beyond rehabilitation for so many years and
washings that the fabric had become thin and soft and
flannel-like. And she remembered the hours of
long, hard work for less than equal pay that she and her
husband had performed in those old rags. She
remembered years on her knees in the vegetable
garden, with children and then grandchildren. She
remembered coaxing a family to eat what was abundant
and free, a product of her own hard work and the
whims of temperature and rainfall—creating wonderful
recipes for great chunks of pumpkin and baskets of
greens. There had been wonderful salads and
creamy soups. There had been pies and breads. She had even
figured out how to hide pumpkin in brownies and
chocolate chip cookies. She wasted nothing,
because the economic realities of her life of exclusion
from the white workforce left her no leeway for loss

or waste or error in judgment when it came to her
slim resources.

After a while, the sheet was out of balance. One end was so
much lighter than the other that she could not throw
it over the big bed in the corner of the room
that held a big woodstove. So she sewed a few more pieces
of old flannel shirtsleeves on to the light end of the
sheet. And by that time, the sheet had consumed
so much labor that it had become a resource that shouldn't
be wasted. So the old woman began to fill in the weak
spots of the ancient flannel fabric, just so it
could support the weight of the newer, heavier used cloths
that increasingly dominated the surface of the sheet.
And, at some point, it became a blanket. And she
kept the prettier side up, turning down the knotted side
with the increasingly ragged flannel base fabric. And
when that flannel base increasingly gave way, she
was compelled to patch that side, too.

Eventually, that blanket was full of memories. When her
husband would come in from working in the barns, he
would point to a patch and remember the comfort
of that particular old shirt. He saw pieces of a
handkerchief with the American flag printed on it that
he had found somewhat stiff and hard to blow his
nose in. He noticed old T-shirts and outgrown children's
clothing and even an old pillowcase cut apart and
stitched wildly in a haphazard fashion throughout

the surface of the increasingly heavy quilt, the vibrant
reds and floral blues distributed evenly, as though
planning had become a part of this crazy fabric
of the life he was sharing with this beautiful woman. And
when one of the grandchildren found her wedding dress
and cut off one of the long sleeves during dress-
up play, he saw the pale flowered fabric spread its way
across the soft quilt that insulated the family every
night. And he remembered her as young and even
more beautiful and enticing. And he remembered unbuttoning
the long row of small buttons on that soft dress and
reaching for the woman inside, kissing her hard,
smiling, and being loved back. He once asked her how she'd
managed to put scissors to the dress, but she'd
answered that the marriage was not about the
dress, it was about the man. Besides, this way she could
still feel its soft fabric against her skin. So could
he.

She made her family biscuits, from scratch. She served them
warm, with wild grape jelly or wild berry jams. And
when children sat on the quilted surface of the
bed where they loved to snuggle, they dropped big gooey
glops of sweetness on the fabric swaths. Their
grandmother would discover the stains, then cover
them with a big circle-shaped patch cut from an old pair of
overalls or a child's T-shirt. And she considered the
growing number of circles a blessing rather than
a chore.

She earned a reputation over the years for her ability to
conserve. And comfortable, middle-class lovers-of-
quilts and conservationists came to her home to
touch the skill and knowledge that manifested itself in
almost everything she touched. She seemed to represent
everything they valued about their new rural
environs in Chippewa country. They came to her for jars of
preserves and fresh vegetables and old-style Indian
dolls made out of cornhusks for next-to-nothing.
And they marveled at her resourcefulness. They wrote with
nostalgia about her skills and talents at conservation
and gardening and gleaning. They begged her to
lend an ethnic presence to their conferences and
educational outreach programs and tributes to
themselves. And they asked her to do these things
for free, even though they themselves drew salaries and
benefits and retirement plans. They never thought
about the fact that they were taking her away
from the endless task of survival in a time and place that
had not allowed her a job in the white working world
for equal pay. And when she suggested payment,
they begged institutional poverty. They espoused the value
of her sparse lifestyle to the fragile planet. They
congratulated her on not using more than her fair
share of resources. And when she spoke of medical and
dental care, they explained how lucky she was to have
any at all, because there were those who were far
needier than she who had far less than them. And when she
opted to save the money she would have to spend on gas
to attend such functions to instead pay her

electric bill, they thought her antisocial. And when she
opted to covet the hours of time she preferred to spend on her
personal needs and those of her family, they
thought her greedy. And when she always chose to stay home
and weed her garden or stitch on her quilt, they
thought of her as someone unwilling to take
responsibility for her community and the futures of its
children. And when she cut a plate-sized circle out of
her wedding dress to cover up the homemade wild
grape jelly stains on the heavy, handmade crazy quilt that
represented her life, they never thought of her as
having been someone's child, having slept under
the soft, pale yellow flannel base fabric that would become
her own future and that of her own children and
grandchildren.

INITIATION

OK, these two Indian women warriors, they walk up the long steps of the
_____ Public Library in Eugene, Oregon. It's a little bit cloudy, and
there's kind of a breeze, but it's warm for early March. And Cinqala is
wearing her favorite blue jacket, the one with a little wolf embroidered
on the pocket. It didn't come that way, but her mom made that little wolf
for her, late at night, when she was done with both of her part-time jobs.
Her mom had tried to find a little wolf pattern at the crafts stores, but
there weren't any. And Cinqala was a pretty good little girl, so her mother
had to get an old birch bark pattern from an old Indian lady that used to
be used for making wolf designs out of porcupine quills. And since most
of the porcupines had been run out of Eugene, Oregon, quite a while ago,
the Indians who still lived there in urban neighborhoods had to use em-
broidery floss. And since Cinqala was a pretty good little girl, she didn't
mind. Because her mom always tries her best.

But those old birch bark quill-working patterns, they're pretty special, and that old lady, she doesn't go around giving them to just anybody.
And now those ogitchidaakweyag, those women warriors, they've asked
Cinqala's mother, would she bring that nine-year-old girl with her next
time they have a sweatlodge. And this is a pretty big deal, so Qala's mother,
she's a little bit nervous, and she squeezes her little girl's hand, and Qala
squeezes back and says, "Don't worry, Mom, I'll take care of you."

Those women warriors, they keep coming, a few at a time, and nobody really notices that they are getting pretty thick back there, on the
second floor, behind the stacks of not-much-used periodicals and a couple of stuffed chairs that don't look like they've been used much either.
They have come from some pretty far places, and they have the perfumes

of different experiences on their clothing and hair. They have the food of exotic diets on their breaths. Their coats are slipped from their bodies and dropped sensuously in a great heap that eventually blocks off entry and visibility to their immediate corner of the world. The coats breathe secrets of a variety of climates and livelihoods. This one is warm and waterproof and smells of fish. This one is stained with house paint. And this one is meant to be worn in public places where the people all dress nice and have money and expect the same of others. One is large and hand sewn from a Pendleton blanket. One is just a vest with pitch and dirt and the scent of pine needles and chain saws. One is light and the color of southerly breezes. And one is small and blue with a wolf embroidered on the pocket.

And those women warriors, they talk softly and laugh quietly and share special stories and jokes and recipes and hugs and soft touches with long fingers. They finger one another's barrettes and admire the quillwork and beadwork on each of them, as well as their ability to constrain the elk and windstorms and wild mustangs and '57 Chevys that want to run screaming from their hair. And the little girl is comfortable and content and wrapped up in the soft smells and the soft sounds and the self-restraint of those women and their barrettes.

The smoke rises from the carpet to the ceiling, thick and lazy, held in by the bookshelves. The women settle in, in a tight circle, welcoming one another's place-confirming touch in the darkness. The heat intensifies, and they welcome the coolness of the short, hard carpet. They say their names in their own native tongues, and they sing clan songs. And those who do not have clan songs, who have had that part of their history and selves stolen away from them, they are given clan songs. They are touched and whispered to and sung to. They are given stories. They share pain. They stroke one another's soft fur. They nuzzle softly at one another's wounds and lick away the poisons and the pus. They cannot see one another's eyes. They can only smell and lick and touch and heal around their small, secret fire.

"What are we going to do about our children's educations?" asks the keeper of the eastern door. It is a question so heavy, so serious, that the warriors have been saving it for last. It is the question that never goes away. It is the uniform scent that lingers on each of the coats and jackets in that doorway-guardian pile at the outside of this space. It is the one thing they sniff for, as each of them enters the sweatlodge prone. It is the staple of all of their varied diets. It is their lives, their nows, their futures.

"Maybe we should write our own books." It is whispered, as though a forbidden topic.

"But who would print the books?"

"Not all books are books. We could write on old bark scrolls."

"We could draw our meanings and histories and stories in sand."

"And each of us could take a handful after each lesson, so that the knowledge will stay with us."

"We could write our stories in songs."

"We already do that."

"We already do all of those things."

"We could teach by example."

"We could whisper truths in love songs and poetry."

"We could do plays."

"We could write new plays, to deal with new problems."

"I know this Cree guy who writes plays," says the keeper of the northern door. "I saw one in a book."

"What library keeps books by Cree guys?"

Ogitchidaakwe is trying to imagine herself going into the small library next to the river in the small white town where the Indians used to live. She is trying to imagine herself asking the tall, thin, unsmiling library lady, "Uh, do you have a copy of *Dry Lips Oughta Move to Kapuskasing*?" And she giggles.

"Do you have any ideas, Cinqala?" asks the keeper of the western door.

"I don't know."

"Do you have any stories to share with us, Qala?" asks the keeper of the southern door.

And Cinqala Huch, age nine, who is in the third grade at Oak Hills School in Eugene, Oregon, shifts on her haunches. She pulls her long gray tail off to the side and smooths it down next to the keeper of the eastern door. She confidently taps her bottom lip with a long claw, and she says, "Weeell. . . . This happened a few months ago, around Thanksgiving. My art teacher, Diane, she made everybody make Indian heads."

The other she-wolves suck in air, quickly, all at once.

"They were little Indian cone things, cylinders made out of yellow paper. They had big three-point noses. She made one cone, and then all the rest of us had to make them. The worst part of all is they had war paint—it was little lightning bolts in red, orange, and yellow. The kids drew and cut out the lightning bolts and pasted the lightning bolts on the faces. She was doing this for Thanksgiving, she said. She was all excited about Indians and pilgrims and day of friendship and blah, blah, blah. Ready, willing, time to go, rapido, rapido. Nobody else had a problem with this."

"Aaaah . . ." the other women sigh, and the room fills with the heavy smell of meat breath.

"Well, I felt very not good, 'cause it was very dyscultural. It was an insult to the culture."

The warriors begin to yip and to scratch at their ears with their hind legs, jostling one another in the cramped space, moving one another like big furry dominoes.

"It was a stereotype," the child continues. "It made me feel insulted."

"Yip, yip, yip, yip," those women call out in support, and that keeper of the eastern door, normally so much in control, she lets out a loud howl.

"Huuushhh . . ." comes the hot meat breath toward the eastern door from all directions within the sweatlodge.

"And I wish that I had never told her I was Indian. I mean, I'm proud of my culture and everything. The whole school knew I was an Indian when I came into the school. I feel fine with my teachers and everything, but I didn't feel comfortable with this.

"I started crying, just because I wanted her to stop."

That keeper of the eastern door, she throws *giishik* into the fire. That keeper of the northern door, she throws *wingaash* into the fire. That keeper of the western door, she throws *maashkideebak* into the fire. That keeper of the southern door, she throws *sema* into the fire. And the rest of those women warriors, they throw hope into the fire, and the future, and good dreams, and moral support, and loving caresses, and kind words; and that hot air in that sweatlodge is pretty thick with all the stuff that a nine-year-old girl needs to get on with being nine years old. There's so much good stuff in that sweatlodge, that that little girl is probably well armed enough with cultural support to make it all the way through age ten, maybe even eleven.

"What happened next?"

"She said right after I had stopped and calmed down, she said to the class, 'If any of you have questions, just ask Qala.' She meant I was her little project. She was just using me as her little teaching tool. She thought that everything she was doing, she knew all about Indians. Everything she was doing was right."

"Hai, hai, hai, hai!"

"Yip, yip, yip, yip!"

"Strong girl!"

"Strong mother!"

The hot meat breath floats all around that little girl. It lifts her up off that cold, hard carpet.

"I guess I would want her to apologize to me personally. In front of my mom, but not the principal. I'd want her to promise she'd never do it again. I'd want her to say, 'Qala, I'm really sorry I did this project in the first place, and that I made you a serious part of it, and that I made you mad. I'll never, ever, ever, ever—twelve evers—do it again.'"

"Hawooo-oo-oo!" the keeper of the eastern door calls out.

"Would you control yourself? We are in a public place!!!" the keeper of the northern door is hissing, and Qala can imagine the woman's lips curled upward above her long, sharp canine teeth, her nose wrinkled, her ears drawn back. In this, she finds comfort.

"I'd say to her, 'Thanks,' and it would be over. I don't know if she'd ever do that again, but I'd check in on her occasionally, around Thanksgiving."

"Heh, heh, heh." Those long doggie noses bob up and down in delight. The whiskers sway. Those women snuffle and lick at one another's ears.

"Maybe we should write down Cinqala's story."

"Maybe we should sing Cinqala's story."

"Maybe we should howl Cinqala's story."

"Not here. This is a public place."

"What better than a public place?"

"Maybe we should do a play about Cinqala's story."

"Maybe we should put Cinqala's story in a book."

"Who's gonna read a book about an Indian girl's story?"

"What library is gonna have a book about Cinqala's story?"

"How about all the libraries?"

"Yip, yip, yip!"

"Welcome to the women's warrior society, Qala." The keeper of the eastern door has rolled over the pup next to her and is nuzzling her tummy.

"I'm really happy that my voice can be heard even though I'm young."

The women smile and pant in unison; and elk and windstorms and wild mustangs and '57 Chevys make one quick circle around the room, before they are tucked behind tight barrettes of beadwork and porcupine quills, and the women warriors slip quietly out the door of the _____ Public Library in Eugene, Oregon. And they leave behind them on the front steps of the building the scents of the four directions and their different experiences and strengths and stories and hopes for the future. And these things will linger on the streets of Eugene, Oregon, like wisps of strength and comfort for many years to come.

THEY'RE DANCIN' UP THERE

The elk are unconstrained, long before those Indian women warriors reach the tiny parking lot. The windstorms have torn loose from their hair, and the seed beads that represent hours of patient labor on beautiful barrettes have been popped from the thread that constrained them as well. They have flown off in every direction, those beads, small projectiles against the gritty gray snow banks of cold March days and nights, beating like sands against the road signs that beg passers-through to slow down for Indian children on the state highway, even though they never do; they are sandblasting the rust off old truck bumpers, pelting the windows of the tribal library like cold hail; they are rolling across ice and asphalt to weed edges and snow-buried, poorly tended auxiliary lawns; and they are beating against the sky, begging for recognition and acknowledgement of the beauty and intensity and deep-seated value of Indian beadwork created lovingly at the tips of long, tired, busy, restless brown fingers.

There are wild mustangs on the pavement, and the passers-through down on the state highway are swerving and braking and cursing the Indians, while the beasts dive and start and turn unexpectedly; '57 Chevys have lined up in the drive-through drop-off lane that goes to the front door of the casino. They are revving their engines. They are blinking their yellow headlights. They move up to the doorway, stop, and drop off no one, before heading up the hills and into the woods, where they are careening on back roads and two-tracks, whooping and honking, circling subdivisions, tearing into lakeside public boat launches, slamming their doors, popping their hoods, blaring out Bobby Vinton and Roy Orbison. They are rearing on their back tires and howling for the moon, those Chevys, even in the middle of the afternoon.

And the bay is swelling, its surface twisted and raucous. The waves are pounding against summer homes and restaurants and private recreational boat slips and marinas. Precious waterfront lots erode and grow smaller. The inherited wealth of homesteaders/usurpers shudders beneath the wind. The boughs of remnant indigenous hazelnuts that have been lying flat under burden of ice and snow now snap back upright and reclaim dead air space. Brittle branches break off from tenuous plantation pines, and skunks seeking spring mates give up their lust and run for cover in burrows and fencerows.

The metal and glass doors of the tribal library snap back with each new human arrival, and the winds sweep through the vestibule, dislodging the freshly restocked brochures for military recruitment of desperate minority youths. Lights flicker, and a desk clock blinks out a hapless red 12:00, 12:00, 12:00. A dark blue pickup truck with rust red highlights backs up to the double doors, and large chunks of old, hollow, well-seasoned cedar are tossed on the concrete slab outside the small metal building. The double doors are propped open with chunks of wood, and the women warriors begin an assembly line, lifting, passing, stacking, until the truck bed is empty and the main room of the library smells of cedar and sweat and hopes and ambition.

There are prayers and expectations and encouragement, and the fire is started with neither match nor plastic lighter, but by the practiced long strokes and encouragement of the keeper of the eastern door. It is blown upon, fanned, sung to, and nurtured from a single spark into a great blaze of determination and intent. And when the room is heavy with smoke, its vents heaving perfume and tradition, those ogitchidaa-kweyag, those women warriors, they hum to themselves softly. At first you can hear a wolf, deep and throaty. But then you can hear those spring peepers. They've climbed up the walls and the bookcases with those little suction-cup toes of theirs, and they're making a racket. Pretty soon those woodcocks jump in, and a bunch of them are flying upward in increasing circles, like males calling for their mates, beeping and twittering, diving in freefall, daring the corrugated metal and sheetrock to constrain them. And a whippoorwill calls out from a dark corner on the hard carpet. And just when you think you can't stand it any longer, those toads jump in, and they puff out their throats and they trill to one another back and forth, back and forth, back and forth across the room so loud that you cover your ears. And the rhythmic, interacting calls and wild, orchestrated motions take away your ability to see or think or feel anything else. . . . You are momentarily captive.

The people who are dodging elk and horses down on the highway hear the thrumming and the loud music, and they curse the Indians, thinking that it is mere low-class rebellion in the form of rock music or defiant style of dress and behavior—the kind that is described in the educational journals written by those who have never been frogs, never been wolves, never been whippoorwills, never sung with frogs, never sung with wolves, never sung with whippoorwills.

You can hear them warriors all the way down to da convenience store. And you know they're up there, lookin' different, singin' different, actin' different, *thinkin'* different. It says so in Educational Sociology 101. They are rebelling against us. They are rebelling against the dominant culture. They are rebelling against the superior culture. They know that they can never be as good as us, so they rebel, they rebel, they rebel.

Think again.

The women warriors are not rebellious. They are merely there. They are not beneath. They are sideways. They are not unique. They are everywhere. They are as ever-present as the turbulence that characterizes the surface of the earth. And they are up there in that tribal library, dancing.

I bet you wanna know how they're dancing up there, don't ya? You wanna know the details. Ya know, there could be a book in it for ya. An article in a scholarly journal, maybe. A doctoral thesis. A career. A life of respect for your research and knowledge.

They're up there in that little tin building waiting for you to discover them. Do you need a guide? Yeah, I know how to be a guide. For a mere two hundred dollars a day, I will be your guide. Meals are extra. Gourmet. Flown in fresh from the grocery store an hour or so away from here. Because this place is wild. This place is scary. This place got deer. This place got foxes. This place got coyotes. This place got bobcats. This place got porcupines. This place got mystical big fish — swallow you whole. This place got shipwrecks. This place got mooountain lions . . . really . . . right next to the 7-Eleven. You can get yourself a frozen Coke, then maybe get clawed to death and eaten up before you can drink it. Right down there on the state highway.

And, hell, that's the *safe* spot. Go up there behind the tribal library, up that unpaved driveway into that nether land between those metal buildings made of poverty, and oh, holy shit, there's spooks and traditions and uncivilization and all sorts of scary shit gonna jump out at you. Spirits. Big motherfucking spirits. Spirits with claws and teeth. Shape shifters. *Women!* Big mean motherfucking nasty Indian women! Women with attitude. Women with children to protect. Women with histories of malcontent. Women with futures to look out for. Women who sing like wolves and toads and wild, swooping birds. Women who dance. . . .

You wanna know how they dance? C'mon, I know you wanna know how they dance inside there, inside that sweatlodge up there. You wanna know what kind of untainted wildness makes those military recruitment brochures come flying out the vents and doors and spreading across that state highway there, being run over by those passers-through, the ones like you, the ones who curse the elk and ponies and defiance and ideas—but are afraid to stop and stare, because they might not be spiritual enough to understand these primal things. You wanna know dem things.

And I'm the one to teach you about them. For maybe a couple hundred bucks a day. And the meals are extra. And if you want a dreamcatcher, that's extra, too.

YOU'RE SO FUCKIN' SPIRITUAL, I CAN FEEL IT

Yeah, they're dancin' up there. You wanna know that dance? Oh, hell, that's easy, I can teach you that dance. I can teach you that dance in a minute. And I can tell that you're gonna be good at learnin' that dance, 'cause you, you look like you got a natural sense of rhythm. Probably got genes for good artwork in there, too—just like them Indians.

OK, you see, it goes like this. First they dance like frogs. Yeah, frogs, that's right. You hear them in there, don't ya? Croakin' like frogs. Don't use nothin' like the notes you're used to, right? Hell, them's animal notes. Animal music, it is. Screeching. Hear them wimen warriors screeching in there? No fucking Beethoven in there. No fucking *Peter and the Wolf* in there. Real wolves in there. Spiritual wolves in there. Mean motherfucking Indian wimen warrior wolves in there. And birds and frogs, and all kinds of shit.

So, you wanna know what they do in there? First they dance like frogs. Really. No shit. They dance like motherfuckin' frogs. Big ol' bowlegged Indian women frogs. They hold hands in a big circle first. And then they wait for the drummers to drum a little bit, until they get the rhythm. Then they bow their legs out like this. Yeah, sideways, like this. And they kinda step sideways like this, in this bent-frog-leg pose like this. Yeah, yeah, like that. . . .

And then they take their shirts off. Oh, you don't wanna take your shirt off? That's OK. Maybe you could just lift your skirt up a little bit. Yeah, like that, that's OK. You're real good at that. You look like one of them wimen warriors. Hell, you look just like fucking Pocahontas. You must be part Indian. Yeah, I bet maybe your great-great-grandma. She was probably like a princess, right? Yeah, she probably never admitted it to nobody, because it wasn't cool back then—not like it is now. Yeah, yeah, you don't need no records . . . you just gotta *feel* like an Indian. You just gotta know how to relate to nature and shit like that. Yeah, it's a good thing you drove up here, 'cause this is a real good place to get next to nature, you know, be like them wimen inside that sweatlodge over there.

You stick with me. I'll give you lessons. Pretty soon, you won't even have to listen to them wimen warriors over there. You won't even need them. You'll be even more Indian than they are. Y'know, they don't even most of 'em even eat organic any more. Really. I mean, they eat genetically modified foods and shit. Really. I mean, they've all got these jobs at the casino and shit, and they don't have time to pick wild berries and shit like you do. I mean, really, you're much, much more Indian than any of them. Hell, they all eat macaroni and cheese out of a box. You know, I like the way you wear your hair all long and straight like that. Did anybody ever tell you that you look like you're part Indian?

I got beadwork at home. Y'know, a little beadwork, and nobody would be able to tell that you're not Indian. No, really, I mean it. You wanna come back to my place, and I'll show you some beadwork? I'll give you a really great price, really, 'cause you're so fuckin' spiritual, I can feel it. We can run into town and get some beer on the way. You got any cash on you? I left my wallet in my feather bustle.

THE DEER DANCE

They are in there. Their children are tappety-tappety-tap-tap-tapping on the computer keyboards in one small cluster. And the women talk among themselves in droning, buzzing voices. Two old women approach the wide glass doors. One holds the door open, while the other shuffles in with a walker.

"Come on in, Dorrie. It's cold out there."

"I don't wan' go in dere. I'd rather just stay home and drink a cup of soup."

"No, come on, the kids brought plenty of food."

"I don't wan' any food. I'd rather just stay home and drink a cup of soup."

"C'mon, we'll go over to the computers, and I'll see if you sent me an e-mail."

"I didn't send any e-mail."

"Well, come on in, and I'll send *you* one."

And those old ladies, they chat and smile their hellos, and pretty soon they've danced over to those computers. Maybe look up some old grave records on those computers. Maybe see the names of someone they love on those computers. Maybe learn about some of the family that they got taken away from when they got taken off to boarding school. Maybe learn some of the Indian language they forgot when they was away at boarding school. Maybe feel some tie to this place that they lost when they was away at boarding school. Maybe stop feeling like they're strangers in this place and don't quite belong, on account of everything having been taken away from them.

This one, she talks about how she lived over near Cedar, grew up there with her parents. No Indians left in Cedar any more. Got run out by the farmers and the homesteaders and the chamber of commerce.

That one, she talks about how her family got run off Old Mission Peninsula onto the Leelanau Peninsula. How they had to make do with less, work things out with the Indians that was already living there. How everybody just tightened up their belts and got along, and how lucky they are that as many of them lived through it as actually did. And she really wants to go home and drink a cup of hot soup.

"No, we're gonna stay here a while, and I'm gonna e-mail you." And that one, she tells her grandson to e-mail ol' Dorrie sitting there next to her. And that grandson thinks that helping these old ladies e-mail each other back and forth next to each other is gonna be a lot more fun than reading about predicate nominatives again and again and again in preparation for the state proficiency exam. And pretty soon his granny calls her other grandson over there, and those two old ladies are really going at it.

"You e-mail Dorrie that there's gonna be a recipe book for the fundraiser over at the health center next month."

"I already know about that cookbook. I gave a recipe for it. E-mail me somethin' else."

"OK, how about I e-mail you what I had for dinner last night?"

"I already know what you had for dinner last night. You told me in the car on the way over."

And the daughters and the mothers are talking and smiling and twittering. And they are nonchalantly building a large bonfire in the back corner of the room, behind the shelves full of children's books about Indians, mostly by non-Indians. Behind the stack of *News From Indian Country* that is sort of out of sight and doesn't get noticed.

The keeper of the eastern door pulls the military recruitment brochures from the table outside the locked office, where they confront every incoming Indian; and she replaces them with stacks of Indian newspapers full of obituaries for Indian military reservists. She throws the recruitment brochures onto the bonfire, where they plop down flatly and cause an acrid smoke. She throws in the heavy cardboard stand-up picture of a marine that holds a pad of mail-in information-request forms, and the marine crinkles and succumbs to the flames, looking a lot less invulnerable than he did on that table facing the door. She pulls the poster from the wall that proudly implies that dying in the military in disproportionate numbers to mainstream culture is "part of your warrior tradition." She tears into long full-color heavy-paper strips that historic requirement that an Indian man must give more than his non-Indian peers in order to be accepted into mainstream society. And she crumples those shreds in her outstretched arms. Her eyes narrow. Her jaw sets hard. She sucks in a long breath through her nostrils, and she screeeams, "Enough!"

"Seymah!" calls out the keeper of the northern door, and sacred herbs are thrown into the fire.

"Seymah!" calls out the keeper of the western door, and sacred herbs are thrown into the fire.

"Seymah!" calls out the keeper of the southern door, and sacred herbs are thrown into the fire.

And the smell of paper and ink is carried off in the updraft.

The women warriors settle in on their haunches and bellies. The frogs and toads cautiously eye the foxes, the wolves, the coyotes, the skunks, the weasels, the frog-and-toad-eating-long-legged birds.

"I can assure you, this is a place of neutrality," an ermine hisses from a band of darkness in the vicinity of the northern doorway. "We all have family here."

And long doggie noses nod in agreement. Skunks and weasels bob their whiskers up and down. Birds of prey tilt their heads to one side and blink an eye. Toad throats swell. And there is a musical refrain. It starts out slow, with just a few whimpers and short barks, a few beeps and trills. Then there are shrieks and long, loud notes that beg for group participation. They are unable to help themselves, those wimen. They are singing so loud that the walls are bulging. The joints that hold together metal and sheetrock and vinyl and window glass are starting to give just a little bit. And smoke is seeping out of those cracks.

Passers-through on the state highway are lifting their noses in suspicion. They feel the thrumming of the music, even though they are trying to drive as quickly as possible through this Indian stain on their white fantasies of Indianlike summer vacations and permanent retirement homes and the notion that they live in a pure, unspoiled piece of nature whose pollution they do not contribute to at all. So they speed up their suvs. Even though there is a sign on the highway that asks them to slow down, because Indian children are walking to and from the gas station and the library and the health center and the houses of their grandmothers and aunties and nieces and nephews. And that smoke from those military recruitment brochures follows those suvs down the state highway, all the way to the grocery store in town. All the way to those white jobs in white schools and white governments and white businesses. The smoke from that pile of business cards from the marine recruiter, it follows those suvs past the casino. The smoke from that pile of business cards from the army recruiter, it follows those suvs all the way past the gas station/convenience store. The smoke from that pile of business cards from the navy recruiter, it follows those suvs all the way past the Indian church with its graveyard full of Indian veterans. The smoke from that pile of business cards from the air force recruiter, it follows those suvs all the way to where the road comes out on the other side of the reservation. And then all that smoke settles out on the bay, where a couple of retired executives from General Motors are ice fishing.

Meanwhile, those wimen warriors, they're dancin' round dat fire. Skunk dancin' with a mouse. Snake dancin' with a frog. Crane dancin' with a whitefish. Wolf tails flashin' all over the place, pokin' everybody in the eyes and noses. Skunk claws scratching up the Formica on those library tables. Herons flapping their wings. Hawks screeching. Dogs howling. Raccoons digging for worms and grubs under that short, hard carpet. Things lookin' pretty wild in that sweatlodge there. Pretty careless. Everybody havin' a good time. Them old ladies e-mailin' each other back and forth. Them grandsons lookin' for a website about farts on the Internet.

And pretty soon, Agodaazhians, the keeper of the library, she comes stompin' in, and she says, "What the hell is going on in here?"

But those skunks, they're busy doin' a mouse dance. And those snakes, they're busy doin' a frog dance. And those cranes, they're busy doin' a whitefish dance. And them wolves is whappin' everybody in the face wit' deir tails. And dem cranes is busy doing crane dancin', so dem wings is flappin' pretty loud. And there's a coupla peregrine falcons flying round the room, screeching real loud. So nobody pays Agodaazhians any attention.

And she says it again, only this time she's shouting, "What the hell is going on in here?"

Only nobody pays any attention to her, 'cause those deer all jump up and say, "Hey, everybody, let's all do a *deer* dance!" So, next thing you know, everybody is dancing in a big circle, with their noses stuck up against each other's butts. There's mice got their noses stuck up skunk butts, and there's frogs with their noses stuck up against some snakes' tails. There's whitefish swimmin' around wit' deir noses stuck up crane butts, grouse with deir bills followin' around coyote butts, mink walkin' around wit' chipmunks stickin' out deir butts. And dem wolves just wavin' deir tails back and forth in everybody's face. Dem wolves got everybody up deir butts. Dem cranes, they're just flappin'. Dem peregrine falcons and dem odder hawks, dey're flyin' too fast fer anybody ta stick deir nose up deir butts.

And dat keeper of da library, she goes over to the drinking fountain, and she tries to fill a Styrofoam cup with water, thinks maybe she's gonna put out dat fire. But them cranes, they're pretty wild, and they keep bumpin' into her and spillin' that cup of water. And that drinking fountain, it's pretty slow, and that fire, it's pretty big. It's all cracklin' and poppin' and makin' just as much noise as dem wimen.

Dat keeper of the library, she stands in the middle of that room. And dem wimen, dey do da deer dance around that angry library keeper. First dey dances to da right, 'cause dey're happy. An' den dey dances to da left, 'cause some of 'em has stuff to be sad about. And den dey dances back to da right, on accounta happy is better than sad. But then they go left again, 'cause dey're havin' such a good time, and then back right, just so's they can give a little bit of an edge to happiness over sadness.

And dat keeper of da library, she puts her hands on her hips, and she hollers, "Who told you that you could do this here?"

And the keeper of the eastern door, she pulls her nose up away from its deer butt, and she says, "Did you hear somethin'?"

And the deer answers, "Naah."

So the keeper of da library, she stomps her foot, and she yells, "*What* are all these spirits doing in here?"

And the keeper of the northern door, she pulls her nose up away from its moose butt, and she says, "Did you hear somethin'?"

And the moose shakes its antlers no.

Then that keeper of da library, she scowls all mean and ugly, and she says, "I'm a Christian, for god's sake!"

And the keeper of the western door, she pulls her nose up away from its badger butt, and she says, "Did you hear somethin'?"

And that badger bares its teeth, says, "Nope."

Pretty soon that Agodaazhians, she's stompin' both her feet. She says, "I'm going to take your federal funding away!"

And the keeper of the southern door, she pulls her nose out of an alligator's butt, and she says, "Did you hear the wind in the trees?"

And that alligator says, "Yeah, yeah, that must be it."

Then that keeper of da library, she stomps out, and dem wimen warriors, dey shout out, "Shut the door! That wind's makin' too much noise!"

UARRIORS AND CHILDREN

OK, these Indian women warriors, they walk into a bar. You visualized a library this time, didn't you? I'm proud of you. You're finally getting it.

Only they don't really walk into a library this time. They just show up at somebody's house for a birthday party for one of their kids. And it's a middle-class house. Maybe not too big. Maybe just right. Maybe not too fancy. Just comfortable.

The children are watching a documentary about how gas bubbles form in the human digestive tract. And they are playing together surprisingly well for ten-year-olds. So the women gather at the kitchen table. They warm their hands against the red candles shining between the bowls of chips and dips. They wrap their fingers around big smooth coffee mugs. They are talking softly, about nothing in particular.

And then the keeper of the eastern door arrives. She backs up her tan pickup truck close to the porch, and she begins to unload boxes of ice candles. The other women are pleasantly surprised, and they help her distribute the delicate globes of ice all around the outside of the house, lighting their small candles with table matches and small plastic cigarette lighters.

"They're so beautiful. How do you make them?"

"It's a cultural secret. If I told you, I'd have to kill you."

"No, really."

"Water balloons. You fill them halfway up with water. Then blow up the other half with air. You prop them up in a snow bank. And when they get a good crust on them, you pop them with a knife. The top freezes flat. Usually the sides are frozen up partway and lacey, and you just pour the water out. Then you flip it over, flat side down, and you add a candle. If the round bottom has frozen shut, just break it with the knife until there's a big enough hole to insert a candle. It keeps the wind off the candle."

The building is surrounded by small, glowing fires, and the cold outdoors does not appear as cold from inside any more. The women warm their fingers against their cups again, and a second pot of coffee is brewed.

"In the old days, they made ice candles out of bladders — from small animals or big fish. They packed them with tallow balls with wicks in them. They used them outside on the lake, when they were ice fishing . . . back when things were a little colder, when there was a longer ice fishing season. They used them to mark weak spots on the ice, too. Sometimes, if they were in a hurry, they just made lamps by pushing the snow up in a ring, but that didn't cast as much light."

"My grandma once showed me this moss that they used to use for wicks. She said that it didn't burn as fast as some of the other plant fibers."

"Yeah, people knew a lot of stuff back then."

"Still do now."

"Yeah."

"That's a nice barrette."

"Thanks. My mother-in-law made it."

And pretty soon, before you know it, them wimen, they got them barrettes pulled out of their hair. And dem elk, and dem windstorms, and dem wild mustangs, and dem '57 Chevys, they take a spin around that house, check out every room, make sure it's safe, ruffle the hair on all them kids watchin' that TV and the ones upstairs playin' see-if-you-can-hit-me-in-the-head-with-that-beanie-baby, and the one sneakin' a finger lick off that birthday cake. Then they go outside, get a good look at them ice candles, see them ladies did a nice job keepin' that tradition goin', and then they cruise the neighborhood, make sure nobody comes stompin' in gettin' upset over a few spirits dancin' and sniffin' each other's orifices. And they stop now and then and they sniff each other's orifices, and they stomp and paw and whinny and rev their engines and knock a few old dead trees across that state road. Make sure nobody disturbs dem wimen 'til they're done wit' dere business.

And when things seem pretty quiet and safe, the keeper of the eastern door, she throws a little giishik onto one of those candles, the one over near the potato chips, and she says, "What are we gonna do about the education of our children?"

And the keeper of the northern door, she says, "Maybe we can't make those military recruiters go away, but we can warn our children about them." Then she throws a little wingaash onto one of those candles, the one over there by the little warm slices of frozen pizza.

And the keeper of the western door, she throws a little maashkideebak onto the candle over by the celery sticks, and she asks, "You got any more milk for this coffee?"

And the keeper of the southern door, she sprinkles a little sema onto one of those candles, and she says, "I think the librarians are getting suspicious."

And the keeper of the eastern door says, "That's OK. There are plenty of other places we can teach our children."

And the keeper of the northern door says, "That's OK. There are plenty of other times we can teach our children."

And the keeper of the western door says, "That's OK. There are plenty of other ways we can teach our children."

And the keeper of the southern door says, "That's OK. There are plenty of other traditions we can teach our children."

And dem wimen warriors, dey sniff and dey wipe hot coffee off dem whiskers wit' dem soft, gray paws. Dey yip a little bit, softly at first, just barely movin' the flames on dem candles on the table and on the kitchen counter between the plates of food. Then one of them pulls a little drum out from under her hooded sweatshirt, and she taps on it, softly, with a long curved claw. And dey sing a soft, sweet song about wolf babies. And them ten-year-olds up there, upstairs, the ones playin' see-if-you-can-hit-me-in-the-head-with-that-beanie-baby, they kinda stomp their feet in a rhythmic way that makes the walls and the ceiling sway. And dem wimen warriors, they start tapping on the tablecloth with both paws, and one of them is shaking a bowl of M&Ms so it sounds like a rattle. . . . So pretty soon them wimen are singing real loud, and yippin' and howlin' for the moon to come out from behind the trees over there where their trucks and old cars are parked behind the old chicken coop. They sing so loud that they blow out those little red candles over there between the chips and the dips. Then the only light in the sweatlodge leaks in through the frosted window glass from those ice candles outside, the ones glowing all around that building.

And the room is filled with meat breath.

ABOUT THE AUTHOR

Lois Beardslee is the author of *Lies to Live By* (Michigan State University Press 2003), *Rachel's Children, Stories from a Contemporary Native American Woman* (AltaMira Press 2004), and *Not Far Away: the Real-life Adventures of Ima Pipiig* (AltaMira Press 2007). She is a contributor to *A Broken Flute, the Native Experience in Books for Children*, winner of a 2006 American Book Award. Beardslee grew up back and forth between northern Michigan and northern Ontario, dividing her time between her extended family's farms and remote bush camps. A lifetime of straddling cultures and traditions (her mother was Ojibwe and her father was Lacandon) has led her to write about the ways in which traditional and modern lifestyles conflict and merge successfully for contemporary Native people. Beardslee writes both fiction and nonfiction and contributes scholarly writings in the fields of multicultural education and literature. She is an adjunct instructor in Communications at Northwestern Michigan College and has a bachelor's degree from Oberlin College and a master's degree from the University of New Mexico.

Beardslee has also been an artist for much of her life, painting, illustrating, and creating rare traditional Ojibwe art forms, including porcupine quillwork, sweetgrass baskets, and birch bark cut-outs and bitings. Her work is in public and private collections worldwide. She continues to divide her time between the family farm and remote bush camps.